This book belongs to:

_____

_____

A Treasury
to Read with
Grandma

This edition published by Parragon Books Ltd in 2017 and distributed by

Parragon Inc.
440 Park Avenue South, 13th Floor
New York, NY 10016
www.parragon.com

Cover illustrated by Rebecca Harry

Illustrated by Deborah Allwright, Lorena Alvarez, Victoria Assanelli, Petra Brown, Livia Coloji, Charlotte Cooke, Ciaran Duffy, Mar Ferrero, Chiara Fiorentino, Beverley Gooding, Katy Hudson, Jenny Jones, John Joven, Russell Julian, Sean Julian, Xuan Le, Emma Levey, Katya Longhi, Polona Lovsin, Davide Ortu, Alessandra Psacharopulo, Kirsten Richards, Loretta Schauer, Gavin Scott, Lisa Sheehan, Christine Tappin, Luisa Uribe, Brenna Vaughan, and Aleksandar Zolotic

Selected stories retold by Claire Sipi
Original stories written by Hans Christian Andersen, David Bedford, Karen Hayles, Rudyard Kipling, Rachel Moss, Anna Sewell, and Margery Williams

Every effort has been made to acknowledge the contributors of this book.
If we have made any errors, we will be pleased to rectify them in future editions.

Designed by Duck Egg Blue
Cover designed by Kate Ford
Edited by Emma Horridge and Becky Wilson

ISBN 978-1-4748-7495-3

Printed in China

A Treasury
to Read with
Grandma

PaRragon

Bath · New York · Cologne · Melbourne · Delhi
Hong Kong · Shenzhen · Singapore

Contents

The Enormous Turnip

Early one spring, a farmer planted a turnip seed. He watered it every day, and soon green shoots appeared above the ground. The seed grew and grew, until the turnip was as big as a pumpkin.

All through the spring, the enormous turnip kept growing and growing.

"Go and pull up that turnip," the farmer's wife said one day. "I want to cook it."

So the farmer went into the field and took hold of the enormous turnip. He pulled and he pulled, but it would not budge.

The farmer called out to his wife. "Can you help me?"

The farmer grabbed the turnip and his wife grabbed him and they pulled and pulled. But still the enormous turnip would not budge.

The wife called out to their son, "Come and help us."

The farmer grabbed the turnip, the wife grabbed the farmer, the son grabbed his mother, and together they pulled and pulled. But still the enormous turnip would not budge.

The son called out to their cat, "Come and help us."

The farmer grabbed the turnip, the wife grabbed the farmer, the son grabbed his mother, the cat grabbed the son, and together they pulled and pulled. But still the enormous turnip would not budge.

The cat saw a mouse running by and called out to her, "Come and help us."

The farmer grabbed the turnip, the wife grabbed the farmer, the son grabbed his mother, the cat grabbed the son, the mouse grabbed the cat's tail, and together they pulled and pulled.

Suddenly, with a loud POP! the enormous turnip came out of the ground.

Everyone cheered, and the wife cooked the turnip, and that evening they all enjoyed a delicious bowl of turnip stew!

The Three Billy Goats Gruff

Long ago, there were three brothers—a little goat, a medium-sized goat, and a big goat.

The brothers lived in a field of short, dry grass beside a river.

On the other side of the river, over a bridge, was a huge meadow with long, juicy grass.

The goats longed to taste the juicy grass, but the bridge was guarded by a horrible, ugly troll.

One day, the little Billy Goat Gruff plucked up his courage and trotted over the bridge.

TRIP TRAP, TRIP TRAP went his feet.

"Who's that TRIP TRAPPING over my bridge?" cried the troll, leaping in front of the little goat. "I will eat you!"

"Please don't!" cried the little goat. "Wait for my brother—he is much bigger and tastier than me."

"All right," said the greedy troll, and he let the little goat cross.

Later that day, the medium-sized goat saw his little brother munching juicy grass on the other side, and wanted to eat it, too.

So he set off, TRIP TRAP, TRIP TRAP, across the bridge.

"Who's that TRIP TRAPPING over my bridge?" cried the troll again. "I will eat you!"

"Please don't!" cried the medium-sized goat. "Wait for my brother—he is much bigger and tastier than me."

The greedy troll licked his lips, and let the medium-sized Billy Goat Gruff cross the bridge.

At last it was the big Billy Goat Gruff's turn to cross the bridge. TRIP TRAP, TRIP TRAP went his hooves on the wooden bridge.

"Who's that TRIP TRAPPING over my bridge?" bellowed the troll, drooling at the sight of the big goat. "I will eat you!"

But the big Billy Goat Gruff was not afraid of the ugly troll.

"You can't eat me!" shouted the big Billy Goat Gruff. He lowered his head, stamped his hooves, and tossed the troll into the river with his great big billy goat horns.

Then the biggest goat went TRIP TRAP, TRIP TRAP over the bridge to join his brothers, and the horrible troll never bothered them again!

The Spider, the Hare, and the Moon

The moon felt very sad. She knew that people on Earth were afraid of the dark, and she wanted to let them know that it was nothing to be scared of. She had no way of speaking to them herself, so she called on her friend the spider.

"Please take a message to everyone on Earth," she said to him. "Tell them that the world will always be in darkness at night, but there is no need to be afraid. I will be here to light their way."

The spider started to climb down the moonbeams to get back down to Earth. On the way, he bumped into the hare.

"Where are you going?" the hare asked.

"The moon has asked me to give an important message to all the people on Earth," the spider explained.

"Oh, you're so slow, it will take you much too long to get there," the hare said. "Let me take the message. I'm much faster than you. I'm sure if the moon said it was important she would want the people to hear it as quickly as possible. Tell me what the message is and I will give it to everyone on Earth."

"Well, I suppose the moon would want the people to hear her message as quickly as possible," the spider agreed. "Tell them the moon said that the world will always be in darkness … "

"Right," said the hare. "Tell the people on Earth that the world will always be in darkness."

And before the spider could finish, the hare had bounded off.

"Wait, wait," the spider shouted after him. "I haven't finished." But the hare had already disappeared.

The spider decided to go back and tell the moon what had happened. Otherwise she would wonder why the people on Earth were still scared.

Meanwhile, on Earth, the hare was busy telling all the people that the world would always be in darkness. And once he had delivered the message, he proudly went back to let the moon know what he had done.

Of course, the moon was furious with the hare—so furious in fact, that she sent him away and wouldn't speak to him ever again.

And the spider? The busy little spider is still trying to carry the moon's message to all the people on Earth as he spins his webs in the corners of our rooms.

No Time

Fall had come, and Scurry the squirrel was in a hurry. All day long, he rushed around collecting and burying nuts ready for the winter.

"Hello, Scurry," squeaked Amelia Mouse. "I've been getting my winter bed ready. It's really comfortable. Come and see."

"No time!" muttered Scurry. "I'm in a hurry."

"Oh," sniffed Amelia.

"Guess what," Walter Woodpecker told his friend. "Today I made my best, biggest tree hole ever. Come and look!"

"No time!" snapped Scurry. "I'm in a hurry."

"Oh," squawked Walter.

"Hey, Scurry! I can dig a burrow faster than anyone in the forest," said Rocky Rabbit. "Come and watch!"

"No time!" yelled Scurry. "I'm in a hurry."

"Oh," sighed Rocky.

That night, as Scurry slept in his cozy tree hole, the wind began to howl. Scurry woke with a start. His house was swaying from side to side, then … CRASH!

"Help!" cried Scurry.

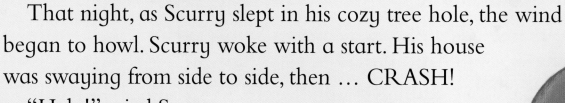

"What's the matter?" called Amelia from her bed.

"My tree's blown over," whimpered Scurry. "Where am I going to sleep?"

"Come and share my warm bed," said Amelia. "There's plenty of space."

"Thank you," said Scurry, quietly.

The next morning, Scurry wept when he saw his damaged home.

"Where will I find a comfortable tree hole like that again?" he cried to his friends.

"Easy!" said Walter. "I told you I'd made a great hole. It'll be perfect for you."

"Thank you," said Scurry, quietly. "But how am I going to move all the nuts? My tree has fallen on top of them."

"No problem," said Rocky. "I can dig them out for you."

When all the hard work was over, Scurry called his friends together.

"Come and have supper in my new home," he said, "as a thank-you for helping me."

"No time!" said his friends. "We're in a hurry."

Scurry hung his head. Then the three friends burst out laughing.

"Oh, Scurry," they said. "We always have time for a friend!"

The Rooster King

Once upon a time, there lived a very boastful king. He was always showing off, but nobody dared say anything because he was the king.

Every day, the king would find something new to show off about, and the queen listened in despair.

"Look at the silly old fool," she would mutter to herself. "Who does he think he is, strutting around like a rooster?"

The story of the king's boastful ways spread throughout his kingdom. One day, an old peddler came to the palace to sell his wares. Of course, he knew all about the king, and he decided to teach him a lesson.

"Your majesty," said the peddler, "I have heard what a fine fellow you are, and I have just the thing for you."

The peddler showed the king a large carved wooden mirror.

"I'll take it," cried the king, who couldn't wait to admire himself in the shiny glass.

But the king didn't know the mirror was magic, and when the vain king looked into it, he was shocked to see a strutting rooster staring back at him.

"This is outrageous!" he started to shout, but all that came out of his mouth was a squawking cock-a-doodle-doo!

The mirror had turned the boastful king into a rooster! He crowed and crowed but no words came out.

When the queen heard the racket, she grabbed the rooster and put him outside the palace.

"Please be quiet!" she scolded the rooster. "It is bad enough that I have to listen to my husband boasting all day, without your dreadful noise too!"

The rooster king hadn't realized what the queen thought of him and he stopped crowing at once.

"If only I can be a man again," he thought sadly, "I promise I will change my boastful ways!"

Suddenly, the king was transformed into a man again. He quickly went back into the palace and locked the mirror away. And from that day on, the king stopped boasting, and he never looked in the magic mirror again!

Scaredy Squirrel

Every day, Ollie would jump out at Annabel and scare her.

"Stop it!" she said one day. "I don't like being surprised."

But Ollie thought it was just a bit of fun. So Annabel decided to show him how she felt. She hid behind a big tree until Ollie came along.

"BOO!" she shouted. Ollie gave a yell and scampered up to the top of the tree.

"That wasn't very nice," he said.

"You always say that being scared is just a bit of fun," Annabel said.

Suddenly, Ollie understood how he had made Annabel feel.

"I'm very sorry," he said. "Will you forgive me?"

"Of course I will," said Annabel, smiling. "Let's be friends."

"I know where there is a secret stash of nuts," said Ollie. "Want to share them with me?"

"That's the kind of surprise I love!" said Annabel. "Let's go!"

The River Rapid Race

Max and Alice were little beavers who loved adventure. One day, they found two hollow logs bobbing at the side of the river.

"Let's race each other!" said Alice. "Bet I'm faster!"

They jumped into the wooden logs and whooshed downstream. At first Max was in the lead, but Alice soon bumped past him.

Faster and faster they both went, and the logs bobbed and wobbled! They weaved between big rocks and water sprayed all around them. Suddenly … CRASH! Alice's log hit a rock.

It turned over and she splashed into the rushing river. Max reached for his friend's paw and pulled her onto his log. They shot out of the rapids and into a calmer part of the river.

"It's a tie!" Max cheered as they bobbed to the bank. "That was super-scary— and super-cool!"

The Velveteen Rabbit

Once upon a time, there was a Velveteen Rabbit made from soft fur, with ears lined with pink satin. When he was given to the Boy on Christmas morning, he was the best present.

At first, the Boy thought the Velveteen Rabbit was wonderful, but then he put him away in the toy chest.

"What is real?" the Velveteen Rabbit asked the toys in the chest one day.

"It's what you become when a child really loves you," explained a hobbyhorse. "I was made real a long time ago by the Boy's uncle. It can take a very long time. By the time you are real some of your fur has dropped out. But it doesn't matter, because once you are real you can't be ugly."

One night, when Nanny was putting the Boy to bed she couldn't find his favorite toy. So she grabbed the Velveteen Rabbit by his ear.

"Here, take your old bunny!" she said. And from that night on, the Velveteen Rabbit slept with the Boy.

At first it was a bit uncomfortable. The Boy would hug him so tightly that the Velveteen Rabbit could hardly breathe. But soon he grew to love sleeping with the Boy. And when the Boy went to sleep, the Rabbit would snuggle down and dream about becoming real.

The Velveteen Rabbit went wherever the Boy went. He had rides in the wheelbarrow and picnics on the grass. He was so happy that he didn't notice that his fur was getting shabby.

One day, the Boy left the Rabbit on the lawn. At bedtime, Nanny came to fetch the Rabbit because the Boy couldn't go to sleep without him.

"Imagine all that fuss about a toy," said Nanny.

"He isn't a toy. He's real!" cried the Boy.

When the Rabbit heard these words he was filled with joy! He was real! The Boy himself had said so.

Late one afternoon, the Boy left the Rabbit in the woods while he went to pick some flowers. Suddenly, two strange creatures appeared. They looked like the Velveteen Rabbit, but they were very fluffy. They were wild rabbits.

"Why don't you come and play with us?" one of them asked.

"I don't want to," said the Velveteen Rabbit. He didn't want to tell them that he couldn't move. But all the time he was longing to dance like them.

One of the wild rabbits danced so close to the Velveteen Rabbit that it brushed against his ear. Then he wrinkled up his nose and jumped backward.

"He doesn't smell right," the wild rabbit cried. "He isn't a rabbit at all! He isn't real!"

"I am real," said the Velveteen Rabbit. "The Boy said so."

Just then, the Boy ran past and the wild rabbits disappeared.

"Come back and play!" called the Velveteen Rabbit. But there was no answer. Finally, the Boy took him home.

A few days later, the Boy fell ill. Nanny and a doctor fussed around his bed. No one took any notice of the Velveteen Rabbit snuggled beneath the blankets.

Then, little by little, the Boy got better. The Rabbit listened to Nanny and the doctor talk. They were going to take the Boy to the beach.

"Hurrah!" thought the Rabbit, who couldn't wait to go, too. But the Velveteen Rabbit was put into a sack and carried to the backyard, ready to be put on the bonfire.

That night, the Boy slept with a new toy for company. Meanwhile, in the backyard, the Velveteen Rabbit was feeling lonely and cold. He wiggled until his head poked out of the sack and looked around. He remembered all the fun he had with the Boy. He thought about the wise hobbyhorse. He wondered what use it was being loved and becoming real if he ended up alone. A real tear trickled down his velvet cheek onto the ground. Then a strange thing happened. A tiny flower sprouted out of the ground. The petals opened, and out flew a tiny fairy.

"Little Rabbit," she said, "I am the Nursery Fairy. When toys are old and worn and children don't need them anymore, I take them away and make them real."

"Wasn't I real before?" asked the Rabbit.

"You were real to the Boy," the Fairy said,

"But now you shall be real to everyone."

The Fairy caught hold of the Velveteen Rabbit and flew with him into the woods where the wild rabbits were playing.

"I've brought you a new playmate," said the Fairy. And she put the Velveteen Rabbit down on the grass.

The little rabbit didn't know what to do. Then something tickled his face and, before he knew what he was doing, he lifted his leg to scratch his nose. He could move! The little rabbit jumped into the air with joy. He was real at last.

How the Kangaroo Got His Tail

Once upon a time, a kangaroo and a wombat lived together in a hut. Back then, kangaroos had no tails and wombats had round heads, so they looked different from the way they do today. Although they enjoyed each other's company, the kangaroo liked to sleep outside and the wombat preferred to sleep indoors.

"Why don't you come and sleep outside with me?" the kangaroo would say. "It's lovely to look at the stars and listen to the sound of the wind in the trees."

"It's too cold and it might rain," the wombat would reply. "I'd much rather sleep in the hut in front of the fire."

As winter approached, the wind became stronger and colder.

"I don't mind a bit of wind," the kangaroo told himself as he huddled up next to a tree, trying to keep warm. Then it began to rain. By the middle of the night the kangaroo felt so frozen, he pushed open the door to the hut and went inside.

"You'll have to sleep in the corner," muttered the sleepy wombat, who was snoozing by the fire. "I don't want you making me all wet."

So the poor kangaroo curled up in the drafty corner, where the rain blew in through a hole in the wall.

In the morning, the kangaroo was cold and grumpy.

"Wake up, you selfish wombat!" he yelled.

The wombat awoke with a start, then tripped and banged his head on the floor, flattening his forehead.

The kangaroo laughed. "That's what you get for not letting me get warm by the fire. Your flat forehead will be a reminder of how badly you treated me last night!"

The wombat was so angry, he picked up a stick and threw it. The stick bounced off the wall and hit the kangaroo, sticking in his backside.

"And from now on that will be your tail!" laughed the wombat. "It serves you right!"

And THAT is why wombats have flat foreheads, and kangaroos have long tails.

The Sick Day

Rabbit felt unwell, so his mother wrapped him up in a fluffy blanket and called Dr. Hare.

"Maybe he has a fever," said Dr. Hare. "Cool him down with carrot salad."

Rabbit's mother made some carrot salad, but Rabbit wasn't hungry.

"Maybe he has a cold," said Dr. Hare. "Warm him up with carrot soup."

Rabbit's mother cooked up a delicious soup, but Rabbit couldn't even eat a spoonful.

"What do you want, Rabbit?" asked Dr. Hare kindly. Rabbit pointed at his mother, who stroked his soft fur and kissed his pink nose. She gave him a big, rabbity cuddle.

"I'm feeling better already," said Rabbit happily.

His mother made him giggle with some funny stories. By bedtime, Rabbit felt well again. His father came home, and Rabbit told him all about the doctor.

"I didn't need salad or soup," he said. "I needed cuddles and funny stories!"

"They're the best medicine of all," said his father wisely.

Oak Tree Hospital

One day, Mrs. Mouse arrived at Oak Tree Hospital in a fluster. "Please help!" she cried. "My son Luca has a thimble stuck on his head!"

The squirrel nurse tried to pull the thimble off, but Luca yelled, "Ouch!" and "Stop!" so she did. The squirrel doctor smeared Luca's head with honey. It made him very sticky and got in his eyes and ears, but it didn't move the thimble one bit. Then the squirrel nurse had a thought.

"Luca, can you waggle your ears and wiggle your eyebrows?" she asked.

Luca waggled and wiggled as hard as he could, while the squirrel nurse and Mrs. Mouse and the squirrel doctor tugged on the thimble. And with a loud POP! the thimble flew into the air and hit the squirrel doctor on the nose.

From then on, just in case, Mrs. Mouse made Luca practice waggling and wiggling every single day—and kept him well away from thimbles!

The Witch in the Woods

Once upon a time, a poor servant girl was traveling through a thick forest with her master and mistress, when she became separated from them and got lost. She walked for hours but couldn't find them. When night fell, the poor girl decided to rest by a big tree.

As she lay on the ground wondering how she would ever find her way home, a white dove flew over to her. He was holding a golden key in his beak.

"See that large tree over there," cooed the dove. "There is a little lock on it. Open it with this key and you will find something to eat and a bed to sleep on."

"Thank you," said the girl, then she gratefully settled down for the night.

The next morning, the dove appeared again. As before, he told the girl to open the lock on the tree. This time, the girl found clothes and jewels fit for a princess.

Every day, the dove did the same. And the girl was provided with everything she needed and more. Although she was lonely in the forest, the girl felt happy and safe.

Then one day, the dove arrived and said, "Will you do me a favor?"

"Of course!" replied the girl. "You have been so kind to me."

"I will lead you to a house," said the dove. "Inside, you will find an old woman asleep by the fireplace and a table full of all kinds of fancy rings. Look for the plainest one you can see and bring it to me as quickly as you can."

The girl followed the dove's instructions, but just as she found the plain ring, the old woman woke up. The girl took the ring and ran out of the house, back to the large tree.

As soon as the girl gave the ring to the dove, he turned into a handsome prince, and the tree became a magnificent castle.

"The old woman is a witch," explained the prince. "She turned me into a dove, and my castle into that tree. You have freed me from the curse. Please do me the honor of becoming my wife."

The girl was overjoyed! She accepted the prince's proposal, and they lived happily ever after.

The Riverbank

The Mole was fed up. "I hate cleaning!" he said, "AND ESPECIALLY spring cleaning!" He slammed the front door of his underground home behind him and raced up the tunnel that led to the open air.

"This is better than whitewashing!" he said to himself as he skipped across toward a river.

Mole had never seen a river before. He sat on the grass and gazed at the water.

"Hello," called a voice from the bank on the other side of the river. It was the Water Rat.

"Hello, Ratty," said the Mole shyly.

"Hello Mr. Mole. Just wait and I'll come across in my boat."

"I've never been in a boat before," said Mole nervously, as he stepped into the boat. "Is it nice?"

"Nice? It's the only thing," said the Water Rat. "Let's make a day of it. We'll have a picnic up the river."

The Mole sighed with contentment and leaned back into the soft cushions. "What lies over THERE?" he asked, waving a paw toward some woods on the far bank of the river.

"Oh, that's the Wild Wood," said Ratty. "We riverbankers don't go there if we can help it. Ah, here's our picnic spot."

They picnicked on the green banks of a backwater, where the weir filled the air with a soothing murmur of sound.

Suddenly a broad, glistening muzzle with white whiskers broke the surface of the water.

"Mr. Otter!" cried Ratty. "Meet my friend Mr. Mole."

"Pleased to meet you," said Otter, shaking his wet coat.

There was a rustling from behind them, and a black-and-white animal with a striped head pushed through a hedge.

"Come on, old Badger!" cried Ratty.

"Hurrummph! Company!" grumbled Badger, and turned his back and disappeared.

"That's just like Badger," explained Ratty. "Hates society."

Just then a racing boat, with a short, round figure inside, splashing badly and rolling a good deal, flashed into view.

"There's Toad!" cried the Otter. Ratty waved. Toad waved and then kept on rowing.

"Oh, dear!" chuckled Ratty.

"It looks like Toad has a new hobby. Once it was sailing. Then it was rafting … then houseboating … and now it's a racing rowboat."

The Otter shook his head.

"It won't last! Whatever Toad takes up, he tires of it and then he starts on something new."

Just then a mayfly swerved overhead and then settled on the river. There was a swirl and a CLOOP!, and the mayfly disappeared. And so did Otter, leaving a streak of bubbles.

The picnic party came to an end, and the afternoon sun was setting as Ratty skulled homeward.

"Ratty! Please, I want to row now!" said Mole, and he seized the oars so suddenly that the Rat fell backward.

"Stop! You'll tip us over!" cried Ratty.

The Mole made a great dig at the water with the oars, missed the surface altogether, and the next moment— SPLOOSH!—the boat capsized.

Oh, dear, how cold the water was, and how very wet it felt! The Mole felt himself sinking down, down, down. How bright and welcome the sun looked as he rose to the surface. How black his despair as he felt himself sinking again—until a paw grabbed him by the neck and he was pulled to the bank.

"Now then, Mr. Mole, trot up and down the path until you're warm and dry again," instructed Ratty.

Meanwhile Ratty rescued the boat, the floating oars, and the cushions, before diving for the picnic basket.

It was a limp and sorry Mole that stepped into the boat.

"Oh, Ratty, can you ever forgive me for my stupidity?"

"Goodness me, dear friend," laughed the Rat.

"What's a little wet to a Water Rat? Don't you think any more about it—we will always be the best of friends. Look here, I really think you had better come and stay with me for a while, and then I'll teach you to row and to swim."

When they got home, Ratty made a fire in the parlor, and found a bathrobe and slippers for the Mole to wear before seating him in a big armchair and telling him stories.

It was a very tired and contented Mole who was taken upstairs to the best bedroom, where he lay his head on a soft pillow and allowed the lap, lap, lap of the river to send him off to sleep. What a busy and wonderful day it had been.

Joey's Favorite Color

One starry night Joey the polar bear cub and his friends were admiring the night sky. It was so colorful that even Joey and his friends were bathed in soft colors.

"Wow, it's beautiful!" gasped Joey.

"I've never seen such a purple sky," exclaimed Hare.

"Purple's my favorite color," said Fox.

"And it's mine too," decided Hare. "What's your favorite color, Joey?"

Joey scratched his head and frowned.

"I don't really know," he said finally. "I've never really thought about it before."

That night, while Joey was asleep, he had a wonderful dream about a rainbow. The rainbow was full of the brightest colors you could imagine. They were so lovely that Joey just couldn't decide which one he liked best.

The next morning, Joey told his mom about his dream.

"I just don't know which color I like best," he told his mom. "How can I decide?"

Mommy Polar Bear laughed. "You don't have to have a favorite color," she said kindly. "I like lots of colors because they make me feel happy."

Joey looked around thoughtfully. He wondered what colors made him feel happy. He loved all the bright colors of the rainbow. But he couldn't decide which color made him feel the happiest.

That evening, as Joey snuggled up beside his mom he felt happy and safe. And all of a sudden he knew what his favorite color was.

It was the color of the snowy world he lived in. It was the color of his two best friends. And, best of all, it was the color of his lovely mom.

Joey's favorite color was white! How could it be anything else?

The Pied Piper of Hamelin

A long time ago, the little town of Hamelin was overrun by rats.

One day, a stranger came to see the mayor. "I will rid your town of rats if you pay me one hundred gold coins," he said.

The mayor agreed and so the stranger began to play an enchanting tune on a pipe. The rats followed the piper, who led them into a river where they drowned. But when the piper went to ask for his money, the mayor refused to pay.

The next day, the piper returned and played his tune again. This time it was not rats that followed him, but children. "When you pay me what you owe, I will return the children," he told the mayor.

The people of Hamelin were furious. "Pay the piper what he is owed," they shouted.

The mayor paid the piper, and the children were returned to their parents.

The people of Hamelin chose a new mayor and, from then on, Hamelin thrived.

The Sun and the Wind

One day, not so long ago, the sun and the wind were having an argument.

"I am stronger than you," said the sun.

"That's nonsense," said the wind. "I am far stronger than you."

"See that man down there?" the sun asked the wind. "I am so strong that I bet I could get that coat off him."

"You're not strong enough to do that," said the wind. "I could easily get that coat off him."

"All right," said the sun. "You go first."

So the wind blew with all his might and strength. Leaves blew off the trees and tiles blew off the rooftops. But the man only pulled his coat more tightly around him. The wind could not get the coat off the man.

"Now it's my turn," said the sun. And he shone down on the man. The strength of the sun was so fierce that the man quickly became very hot. He became so hot that he took off his coat and slung it over his shoulder.

"I win!" said the sun.

"Oh, blow!" said the wind.

Blossom the Cow

Blossom the cow lived on a big farm at the top of a hill. Sometimes visitors came to stay at the farm on vacation. Mrs. Pinstripe, the farmer's wife, looked after the guests while her husband, the farmer, looked after the animals.

One Monday morning, Mrs. Pinstripe noticed that none of her guests had eaten their breakfast.

"Is anything wrong?" Mrs. Pinstripe asked them.

"Umm, well, the butter and milk taste funny," said one guest.

"And the yogurt," said another.

"How odd! Yesterday's milk was fine," Mrs. Pinstripe told her husband. "It must be Blossom."

But Blossom had always won prizes for her milk because it was so tasty. What could be wrong?

All that day, and for the rest of the week, the farmer watched Blossom eat grass. Every evening, after milking her, he tasted the milk. It was lovely and sweet.

On Sunday, Blossom seemed very excited. As soon as the farmer let her into the field, she went straight to the stream and waited.

Soon, a group of children walked into the field and laid a large rug on the grass next to Blossom. Then they started to eat from their picnic basket. Every time they offered Blossom something, she turned her head away, until she saw … CHIPS! Onion-flavored, spicy barbecue-flavored, cheddar and sour cream-flavored—any flavor with a strong taste!

The farmer was amazed. "So that's why her milk tastes strange!" he said.

The next Sunday evening, after another picnic with the children, the farmer gave Blossom a handful of extra-strong peppermints. Then, he waited a while for the minty flavor to go into her milk.

On Monday morning, Mrs. Pinstripe watched as her guests ate and drank everything. Then they asked for more!

"Mrs. Pinstripe," said one of the guests, "this peppermint-flavored yogurt is delicious."

Mrs. Pinstripe smiled at her husband and whispered, "If only they knew."

Ebony

Once upon a time there was a beautiful young horse called Ebony. He was as black as midnight, with a white star in the middle of his forehead. Ebony was the only black horse in his herd and was very proud of his good looks.

Ebony lived on a wild moor with the rest of the herd. They had a wonderful life roaming free. They would gallop through the bogs, munch on plants, and do exactly as they pleased. Ebony should have been very happy, but he was always dreaming of a better life.

"I'm so handsome," he would boast. "I feel sure that I am destined for better things."

One day, Ebony saw a grand coach passing by. It was pulled by four black horses—but not one of them was as handsome as Ebony.

"What a fine thing it would be to pull a coach like that," sighed Ebony, as he watched the coach pass by.

Suddenly, Ebony had an idea. He would follow the coach and see if he could make friends with the four black horses who pulled it. Maybe they could tell him how to become a fine horse like them.

So, with a brief neigh, Ebony wished farewell to the rest of the herd and trotted off down the road.

Ebony followed the coach and horses until they reached a small village, where he was soon spotted by a country farmer who was passing by.

"What a beautiful creature," exclaimed the farmer, who was called Farmer Jones. And he quickly caught the wild horse and took him home.

Ebony was turned out into a small paddock with an old carthorse called Fred, and his new life—and his training— began. Before long he was pulling his new master and his family in a small trap.

Of course, it wasn't the fine coach Ebony had dreamt of, and Ebony was still sure he was destined for better things, but he enjoyed pulling the trap and sharing the paddock with Fred— even if the old carthorse was a little on the rough side.

After Ebony had been pulling the trap for some months, a saddle was put on his back for the first time, and he was broken to ride. After that, he regularly took Farmer Jones into market. But the thing Ebony loved best was taking Farmer Jones hunting, and he soon became one of the finest horses in the county. He could gallop faster than any other, and jump higher than most. He was so handsome and powerful that he was admired by everyone.

One day, a fine coach pulled up outside the farm and a well-dressed gentleman and noisy girl jumped out. They had heard about Ebony, and had come to buy him for a large bag of gold. Ebony was thrilled. Now at last he would live the life he deserved!

Ebony was taken to a grand house. At first he was excited, but when he saw his new home he was shocked. It was a dark and dirty stable. His stablemates, who pulled the fine coach, were so grumpy that really he only had the rats for company.

Every day, Ebony was taken out of the stable and a hard saddle was thumped on his back. Then the noisy girl would leap onto his back. She would yank him in the mouth and thump him in the sides with her sharp heels. Then she would gallop him without mercy and jump him over everything from rusty barbed wire fences to long-forgotten plows.

The years passed and Ebony changed. He grew skinny and his fine black coat lost its shine. He could no longer gallop and jump as he had before. One day, the noisy young girl decided she didn't like him any more.

"I want a new horse," she told her father.

So Ebony was sent to market, where no one gave him a second glance.

Luckily for Ebony, a familiar figure appeared before the end of the day and rubbed him on the head. It was Farmer Jones. The kind farmer bought Ebony for just a few silver coins and led him away. But he didn't take him back to the farm. Instead, he led Ebony up to a wild place and let him go.

At first Ebony was scared, but then he saw a familiar rock. He sniffed the air and looked around him. In the distance he could see a herd of horses. He neighed and one of the horses neighed back. Ebony kicked up his heels and galloped away from Farmer Jones. He was home at last. And after all his adventures, he finally knew that the wild moors were the best place in the world.

The Lion and the Mouse

Once upon a time, there was a huge lion who lived in a dark den in the middle of the jungle. If Lion didn't get enough sleep, he became extremely grumpy.

One day, while Lion lay sleeping as usual, a little mouse thought he'd take a shortcut home straight through the lion's den.

"He's snoring so loudly," thought Mouse. "He'll never hear me."

But as he hurried past, he accidentally ran over Lion's paw.

"How dare you wake me up!" Lion roared angrily, grabbing the mouse. "I will eat you for my supper."

"Please," cried Mouse. "I didn't mean to wake you up. I'm too small to make a good meal for someone as mighty as you. Let me go and I promise to help you one day."

Lion laughed loudly. "You're too small to help someone as big as me," he said scornfully, but he opened his paw. "Go home, little mouse."

Mouse looked at Lion in surprise.

"You have made me laugh, so I will let you go," Lion explained. "But hurry, before I change my mind."

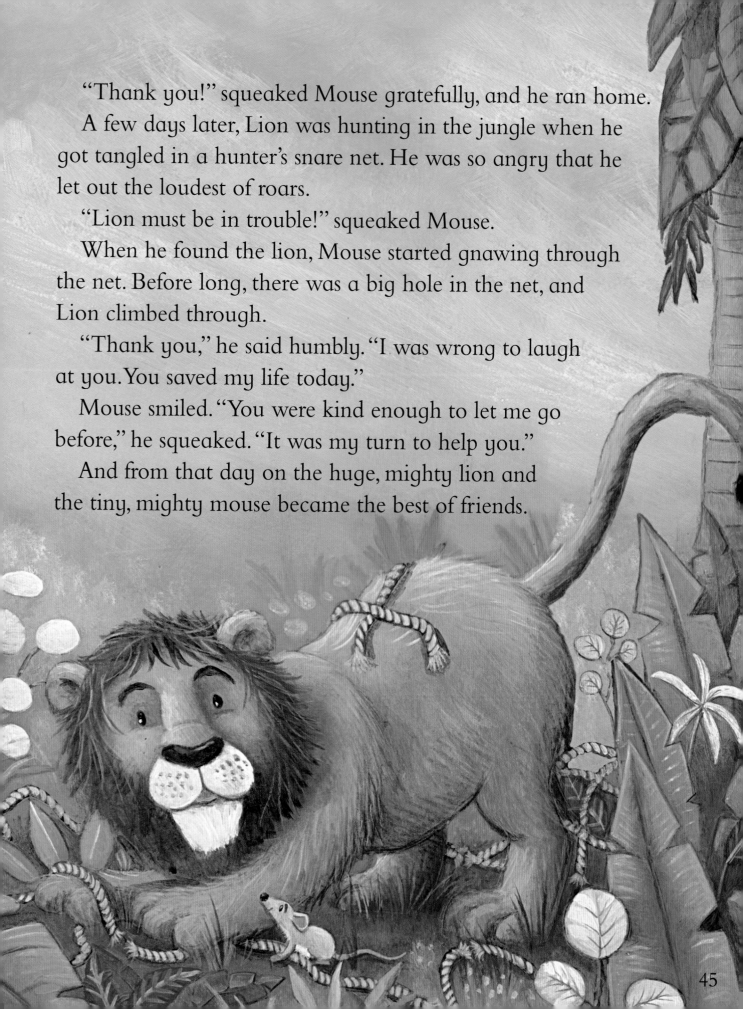

"Thank you!" squeaked Mouse gratefully, and he ran home.

A few days later, Lion was hunting in the jungle when he got tangled in a hunter's snare net. He was so angry that he let out the loudest of roars.

"Lion must be in trouble!" squeaked Mouse.

When he found the lion, Mouse started gnawing through the net. Before long, there was a big hole in the net, and Lion climbed through.

"Thank you," he said humbly. "I was wrong to laugh at you. You saved my life today."

Mouse smiled. "You were kind enough to let me go before," he squeaked. "It was my turn to help you."

And from that day on the huge, mighty lion and the tiny, mighty mouse became the best of friends.

The Stolen Plow

In a place, far away, there lived two merchants who were the best of friends. One lived in a village and the other lived in a town.

The village merchant had a broken plow, so he took it to the town and left it with his friend, who had promised to get it repaired. But the town merchant sold the plow instead and kept the money for himself.

Eventually, the village merchant decided to go and get his plow back.

"I'm so sorry," said the town merchant. "Mice ate your plow!"

The village merchant didn't believe that mice could eat a metal plow, but he kept quiet.

"Never mind, my friend," he said, hatching a cunning plan. "These things happen. It's such a hot day—I think I might go swimming in the town lake. Could I borrow your horse and cart to get there?"

The town merchant was relieved that his friend believed the story, so he willingly agreed, and the village merchant went to the lake.

46

Once there, he hid the cart and returned to his friend's house with the horse.

"I'm so sorry!" he cried. "While I was swimming, a big bird grabbed your cart and flew away!"

"That's impossible!" shouted the town merchant. "I want my cart back. I will take you to court."

When the judge heard the story, he told the village merchant that he didn't believe that a bird could carry off a heavy cart.

"Your honor," replied the village merchant calmly. "If mice can eat through a metal plow, a bird can fly away with a cart."

"What do you mean by that?" asked the judge.

The village merchant told him the whole story. When he had finished, the judge turned to the town merchant.

"You have cheated your friend," he said. "You must replace his plow and then he will return your cart to you."

The greedy town merchant knew he was in the wrong. He bought his friend a new plow, and never cheated him again.

Jungle Hide-and-Go-Seek

One day Little Elephant was walking through the jungle. He hadn't gone far when he bumped into Giraffe.

"Hello," called Little Elephant. "Do you want to play?"

Giraffe peered down at Little Elephant and smiled.

"Okay," he said. "You can play hide-and-go-seek with me, Zebra, and Crocodile. Close your eyes and count to one hundred, then come and find us."

So Little Elephant closed his eyes and counted to one hundred, which took a very long time because he was only a very little elephant. Finally, he opened his eyes and began to search the jungle for his friends.

He searched through the long grass, but he didn't see Zebra hiding among the tall blades. He searched among the acacia trees, but he didn't see Giraffe hiding between the tree trunks. He searched the watering hole, but he didn't see Crocodile hiding in the shallows. He searched and searched but he couldn't find any of his friends. By midday, Elephant was feeling so sad that he decided to call it a day.

"I give up," he shouted. "You are all too good at hiding for me."

Then he lay down among some rocks to rest.

One by one, Giraffe, Zebra, and Crocodile crept out of their hiding places and went in search of Little Elephant. But they couldn't find him anywhere.

They made so much noise stomping around that Little Elephant woke up and groaned.

"Hey, that rock just groaned," gasped Giraffe.

"I'm not a rock," said Little Elephant. "It's me, Little Elephant."

"So it is!" cried Zebra.

"That's amazing," smiled Crocodile. "Your gray skin makes it hard to see you when you are hiding among the rocks. Just as my green skin helps me to hide in the watering hole."

"And my stripes help me hide in the long grass," said Zebra.

"And my patches help me hide among the tall trees," said Giraffe.

"Hooray," cried Little Elephant happily. "I'm good at hiding—just like you!"

One Bear Lost

Ten sleepy bears wake from a winter's night.
One wanders out in the early morning light.
Nine scruffy bears wash in a sparkling stream.
One dries off, his fur all fresh and clean.
Eight hungry bears go on a hunt for food.
One wanders off when she smells something good!
Seven silent bears pad softly through the trees.
One sniffs some honey and goes looking for bees.
Six bears have fun in the snow.
One disappears—bottom high, head low.
Five strong bears climb up a slippery slope.
One slides down. She let go of the rope!
Four weary bears take a rest at the top.
One falls over, flippety-flop!
Three lively bears slide down the icy hill.
One stops to rest, calm and still.
Two brave bears paddle, steady and slow.

One gets stranded. Where should he go?
Nine weary bears have gone back home.
But look! One poor bear's left all alone.
One bear lost!
Nine worried bears call out for their friend.
Ten happy bears are back together again.
Ten tired bears are fast asleep in their cozy den.

The Ugly Duckling

Once there was a proud and happy duck. "I have seven beautiful eggs and soon I will have seven beautiful ducklings," she told her friends on the riverbank.

A while later she heard a CRACK! One beautiful duckling popped her little head out of a shell. And then another … and another … until she had six beautiful little ducklings, drying their fluffy yellow wings in the spring air.

"Just one egg left," quacked Mother Duck, "and it's a big one!"

For a while, nothing happened. Then, at last, the big egg began to hatch.

Tap, tap, tap! Out came a beak.

Crack, crack, crack! Out popped a head.

Crunch, crunch, crunch! Out came the last duckling.

"Oh, my!" gasped Mother Duck, "Isn't he … different?"

The last little duckling did look strange. He was bigger than the other ducklings and he didn't have such lovely yellow feathers.

"That's okay," said Mother Duck. "You may look different, but you're special to me."

When Mother Duck took her little ducklings for a swim, each one landed in the river with a little plop. But the ugly duckling fell over his big feet and landed in the water with a big SPLASH! The other ducklings laughed at their clumsy brother.

"Hush now, little chicks," said Mother Duck. "Stick together and stay behind me!"

Back at the nest, the ducklings practiced their quacking.

"Quack, quack, quackety-quack!" said the ducklings, repeating after Mother Duck.

"Honk! Honk!" called the ugly duckling.

The other ducklings all quacked with laughter.

The ugly duckling hung his head in shame.

"I'll never fit in," he thought sadly.

The next day, Mother Duck took her little ones out for another swim. The little ducklings stayed close to her while the ugly duckling swam alone.

"What kind of a bird are you?" asked some geese, who had landed on the river nearby.

"I'm a duckling," he replied. "My family has left me all alone."

The geese felt sorry for the ugly duckling, and asked him to go with them. But the ugly duckling was too afraid to leave his river, so he stayed put.

When Mother Duck wasn't looking, the other ducklings teased their ugly brother.

"Look at his dull, gray feathers," said one of his sisters unkindly, admiring her own reflection in the water. "Mine are so much prettier."

The ugly duckling swam away and looked at his reflection.

"I don't look the same as them," he thought, sadly.

So he swam down the river and didn't stop until he'd reached a place he had never seen before. "I'll stay here," he decided.

Summer turned to Fall. The sky became cloudy and the river murky. But still the ugly duckling swam alone in his quiet part of the river.

Snow fell heavily that winter and the ugly duckling was cold and lonely. The river was frozen solid.

"At least I can't see my ugly reflection any more," he thought.

Spring arrived at last and the ice thawed.

Some magnificent white ducks arrived on the river, and swam toward the ugly duckling.

"You're very big ducks," he said, nervously.

"We're not ducks," laughed the elegant creatures. "We're swans—just like you!"

Puzzled, the ugly duckling looked at his reflection in the river and was surprised to see beautiful white feathers and an elegant long neck.

"Is that really me?" he asked.

"Of course," they told him. "You are a truly handsome swan!"

The handsome young swan joined his new friends and glided gracefully back up the river with them.

When he swam past a family of ducks, Mother Duck recognized her ugly duckling straightaway. "I always knew he was special," she said.

And the beautiful young swan swam down the river proudly, ruffling his spectacular white feathers and holding his elegant head high.

Frog Goes Exploring

Frog had lived happily on the riverbank for so long that he was friends with everyone—from the smallest minnow to the finest swan. He couldn't wish for a better place to live. But Frog had a secret dream. He dreamed of finding out where the river went. He imagined that it led somewhere exciting—perhaps a great city or an exotic jungle, or maybe a sunny beach.

So one winter, Frog got to work building himself a boat. He sawed and hammered all winter long, and by the spring his boat was ready.

After waving goodbye to all his friends, Frog set off on his great adventure. He hadn't been rowing for long when a head popped out of the river.

"Where are you going?" asked the fish.

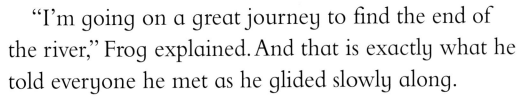

"I'm going on a great journey to find the end of the river," Frog explained. And that is exactly what he told everyone he met as he glided slowly along.

All day, Frog rowed down the river, having a wonderful time. The sun shone down, and birds and animals called hello to him. He passed open fields, small villages, and great towns. There was so much to see that Frog barely noticed the miles going by, and he never thought about stopping for a rest. On and on he rowed until, suddenly, he stopped with a THUD! The boat had hit dry land, and his journey was over!

Frog looked around with excitement. What fabulous place had he found? But he wasn't greeted by the sight of a grand city or a towering jungle, or even a busy beach. He hadn't arrived at a fabulous place. He had arrived at a small pond.

It wasn't at all what Frog had expected. But he wasn't disappointed. He waved to a friendly bluebird, and called hello to a curious bee. Then he sat back and smiled.

"I've had a wonderful day," he thought. "I've seen lots of lovely things and met so many nice creatures. I guess it's not where you are going but how you get there that is most important!"

The Wolf and the Clever Lamb

One afternoon, a little lamb was munching on some grass when she felt thirsty. So she wandered away from her flock to search for some water. Before long, the lamb found a freshwater spring and started to drink from it.

Meanwhile, a big bad wolf was prowling around. He spotted the lamb by the spring and licked his lips greedily.

"This is a lucky day for me!" he growled.

The wolf called out to the lamb, "Little lamb, this spring belongs to me. You have made the water dirty by drinking from it. How will I drink it now?"

"Dear sir, the spring flows from where you are standing," replied the lamb. "And I'm standing downstream, so I cannot possibly dirty your water."

The hungry wolf had not been expecting such a smart answer. "Well, I will eat you anyway!" he cried, and he pounced on the lamb.

But the lamb, being a clever creature, had an idea.

"I have just eaten a lot of grass," she said, "and I'm feeling rather full. If you eat me now you might get a tummy ache from all the grass inside my stomach."

"Well, what should we do?" asked the wolf impatiently.

"If I dance and jump around, the exercise will help me to digest the grass more quickly," replied the lamb, and she started to move.

As the lamb danced and jumped, the bell around her neck began to ring. And the more she moved, the louder it rang. The shepherd, who was looking for the missing lamb, heard the bell, and came rushing to the spring. When the wolf saw the shepherd, he ran away as fast as he could. Later, the clever little lamb told the rest of her flock how she had outsmarted the big bad wolf!

Kind Crane

Crane worked hard on the railroad, but the snooty train ignored him. "I don't speak to lowly cranes," she said.

One day, the engineer was late. "I don't need him," said the train. "I can drive myself." She pushed forward and set off toward the station. But she didn't notice a rock on the track. CRASH! She hit the rock and was knocked onto her side, with her wheels spinning. "Help!" she cried.

Crane bent down toward her. He used his hook and chain to gently lift her back onto her wheels. Then he knocked the rock from the track and pulled her back into position.

"Thank you," said the train. "But why are you helping me?"

"I think it's important to be kind," said Crane. The train felt bad. She knew that she hadn't been kind.

"I'm very sorry," she said. "From now on, we're a team!"

The Ocean Emperor

Santino had been fishing all day. "I haven't caught anything!" he shouted. "I'm not leaving without a fish!"

The sea creatures gathered underwater. "Let's show him what we can do," said the crab. Jellyfish leaped out of the water. Dolphins hopped across the waves on their tail fins, balancing crabs on their noses.

"Help!" Santino yelled as an octopus tried to climb into his boat. "Please don't eat me!" He stared at the beautiful sea creatures that were dancing and splashing around his boat. "Oh I see," he exclaimed. "You don't want to me to catch you because you don't want to be eaten either!"

Santino smiled and put away his fishing net. "I will never try to catch you again," he promised. "Keep dancing in the sea, where you belong!"

The Fox's Tail

One day, a fox was out walking when he heard a loud snap and felt a sudden pain in his tail. The poor fox had been caught in a hunter's trap. He looked behind him and saw that his tail was completely stuck. No matter how much he struggled, he just couldn't free it.

"Help!" he shouted. "Ouch!" he cried. "Owwww!" he howled. But no one came to help him.

At last, the fox pulled and pulled with all his strength and managed to break free, but when he looked back, he saw that his tail had been left behind in the jaws of the trap.

"What will all the other foxes think when they see me?" thought the fox. "They'll all laugh at me. I don't even look like a fox without my tail. It's so embarrassing!"

For days the fox hid away in his den and only came out at night when no one could see him. Then he came up with an idea. He called a meeting of all the foxes in the area.

The foxes gathered in a clearing. Sure enough, as soon as they saw the fox without his tail, they started to laugh.

"I've called you together to tell you about my wonderful discovery," the fox announced, struggling to be heard above their laughter. "Over the years, I've felt that my tail was nothing but a nuisance. It was always getting muddy, and when it rained it got all wet and took ages to dry. It slowed me down when I was hunting, and I never knew what to do with it when I was lying down. So I decided it was time to get rid of it, and I can't tell you how much easier it is to move around without all that extra weight dragging along behind me. I cut my tail off, and I recommend that you all follow my example and do the same."

One of the older foxes stood up. "If I had lost my tail like you, I might have agreed with what you are saying," he said. "But until such a thing happens, I will be very happy to keep my tail, and I am sure everyone else here feels the same."

The other foxes all stood up and proudly waved their tails in the air as they walked away.

And the moral of the story is: do not listen to the advice of someone who is trying to bring you down to their level.

Why the Sea is Salty

Once upon a time there were two brothers, one rich and one poor. The day came when the poor brother had no food left in his house and so he went to his rich brother to beg him for something to eat.

The rich brother was not happy about this, but he said, "I will give you this ham, but you must go straight to Dead Man's Hall."

The poor brother was so grateful for the food that he agreed to his brother's request.

He walked and walked all day. It was just getting dark when he came to a large building. There was an old man outside, chopping wood.

"Excuse me, kind sir," said the brother. "I am going to Dead Man's Hall. Am I on the right track?"

"Oh, yes!" replied the old man. "You are here. When you go inside, the people there will want to buy your ham. Don't sell it to them unless they give you the hand mill which stands behind the door."

The brother thanked the old man for his advice, and went into the hall. Everything happened just as the old man had said it would. The brother left the hall with the hand mill. He asked the old man how it worked and then set off home.

Now the hand mill was magic. When the brother got home, he ground a feast of food and drink for himself and his wife. Whenever they needed anything, they just had to grind the mill.

When the rich brother saw that his brother was no longer poor, he became jealous and angry.

"You must give me that mill," he insisted when he saw what it could do. The brother had everything he needed, so he sold the mill to his rich brother, but he did not tell him how to stop it grinding.

When the rich brother got the mill home, he immediately asked it to grind lots of food. But because he didn't know how to stop it, the mill carried on grinding food until it was flowing out of the house and across the fields. He ran to his brother's house.

"Please take it back!" he cried. "If it doesn't stop grinding soon the whole town will be destroyed."

So the brother took it back, and was never poor
or hungry again.

Soon the story of the wonderful magic mill
spread far and wide.

One day a trading sailor knocked at the brother's door.

"Does the mill grind salt?" he asked.

"Of course," replied the brother. "It will grind
whatever you ask it."

The sailor was desperate to have the mill
so that he wouldn't have to sail far
away over the perilous sea to buy
the bags of salt he traded.

"I will give you a thousand coins for the mill," cried the sailor.

At first the brother was reluctant to sell it, but then he decided that he had gained more than enough from it, so he agreed.

The sailor was in such a hurry to leave and try the mill out, that he forgot to ask the brother how to stop it grinding. When he had gone a little way out to sea, he put the mill on deck and said, "Grind salt, and grind both quickly and well."

Of course, the mill did his bidding, but it didn't stop. The heap of salt grew bigger and bigger, until at last the ship sank under the weight of it.

The mill still lies at the bottom of the sea to this day. And day by day, it grinds on and on, and that is why the sea is salty.

The Cowardly Lion

Once upon a time there was a lion called Saber. Saber looked just like other lions. He had a big shaggy mane, huge powerful claws, and teeth like daggers. And just like other lions, the whole jungle rumbled when he roared. But Saber wasn't actually like other lions at all. He wasn't fierce and scary—he was a cowardly lion. When other animals challenged him to a fight, he simply fiddled with his tail and looked silly.

Even the dogs from the nearby village laughed at him. Poor old Saber felt very lonely.

Then one day, as Saber was walking through the jungle, a terrible thing happened. Something flickered in the undergrowth and then flames began to leap out of the trees. A herd of elephants charged past, heading for the safety of the watering hole. More and more animals joined the stampede. Only Saber and one of the dogs from the village stayed where they were.

"Help," barked the dog. "My puppy is back there in the fire."

Saber didn't wait to hear more. He gave a great ROAR and leaped into the flames. Moments later, he was back holding a small black bundle in his gentle jaws. He dropped the puppy beside its mother and raced down to the waterhole. But he didn't stay long. He gulped down a mouthful of water and rushed back to the flames.

All the other animals watched in amazement as Saber spat the water into the fire. What was he doing?

Suddenly, the elephants realized what he was trying to do. Saber was trying to put out the fire. He was trying to save the jungle!

One by one, the elephants joined in, using their trunks to squirt water at the flames. Before long, the fire was out. Thanks to Saber, the puppy and the jungle had been saved.

At long last, the other animals realized that Saber wasn't a cowardly lion after all. He was a very brave lion. A very brave lion, who just didn't like fighting!

Rikki-Tikki-Tavi

Rikki-Tikki-Tavi was a small furry mongoose. He lived a happy life with his parents in the jungle. Then one day, a great summer flood washed him from his burrow. He was swept into a roadside ditch.

When he revived, Rikki-Tikki-Tavi was lying in the middle of a path in front of a house.

"Look, Mom! A mongoose," cried a young boy.

"The poor little thing is exhausted," said the boy's mother. "Let's take him in to dry."

The little boy was named Teddy and he lived in the house with his parents. The family were so kind that Rikki-Tikki-Tavi decided to stay.

One day when Rikki-Tikki-Tavi was exploring the yard, he heard somebody crying. It was Darzee the tailorbird and his wife.

"What's the matter?" asked Rikki-Tikki-Tavi.

"Nag, the black cobra, has eaten one of our babies," sobbed Darzee, as a hideous snake slithered into sight.

"I'm Nag," hissed the snake. "Be very afraid."

Rikki-Tikki-Tavi did feel afraid, but he knew it was every brave mongoose's duty to fight deadly snakes. He held his little tail high and puffed out his cheeks. He looked terrifying and Nag began to shake.

"Watch out behind you!" cried Darzee.

Nagaina, Nag's wicked wife, had crept up behind Rikki-Tikki-Tavi. He leaped into the air and just missed being struck by her. The two snakes slithered off into the tall grass.

"I'm going to need all my strength to fight Nag and his wife," said Rikki-Tikki-Tavi. "I must protect my new family and friends."

That night, when Teddy was safely asleep in bed, Rikki-Tikki-Tavi crept out into the yard. He could hear Nag and Nagaina whispering in a dark corner.

"We'll bite the big man first," hissed Nag. "Once the humans are gone, that mongoose will have to go."

"Yes," agreed his wife. "We'll need the space in the yard as soon as our eggs in the melon bed hatch."

Rikki-Tikki-Tavi shook with rage at hearing this, but he hid as the giant cobra slithered into the bathroom, ready to bite Teddy's father in the morning.

As soon as Nag fell asleep, Rikki-Tikki-Tavi pounced. He sank his fangs into the cobra's head and held on as the huge snake thrashed around. Rikki-Tikki-Tavi was sure he was going to be beaten to death. Then, suddenly, a gun went off and Nag was no more. Teddy's father had heard the noise and now he had shot the wicked snake.

"Thank you!" he cried. "You saved our lives."

Rikki-Tikki-Tavi felt very pleased with himself, but he knew he still had to deal with Nagaina.

The next day he ran into the yard.

"Darzee, I need you to distract Nagaina for me," he cried.

As soon as the coast was clear, Rikki-Tikki-Tavi rushed to the cobra's nest and began to smash the eggs. He had just picked up the last egg when Darzee started to scream.

"Quick!" he cried. "Nagaina is going to hurt Teddy!"

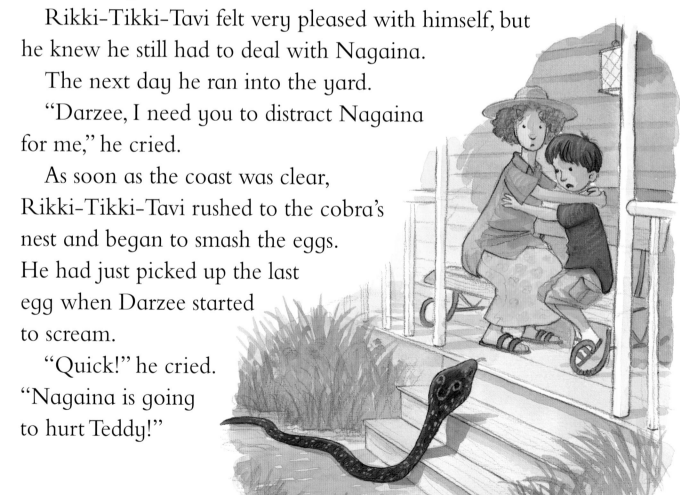

Rikki-Tikki-Tavi rushed up to the house. Nagaina was coiled, ready to strike Teddy.

"Stop!" shouted Rikki-Tikki-Tavi. "I've smashed all your eggs. This is the last one."

Nagaina sprang at the mongoose. She snatched the egg and rushed into her burrow.

Rikki-Tikki-Tavi just had time to grab her tail. He followed her into the dark burrow.

Darzee held his breath. "Oh, this is not good."

But a few minutes later, the mongoose appeared.

"It's all over," he said proudly. "The cobras are dead."

"You saved our lives again!" cried Teddy's mother.

And that's the last time a cobra ever dared set foot inside the walls of Rikki-Tikki Tavi's yard!

The Brahmin, the Thief, and the Giant

Long ago, there lived a wise and kind Brahmin. He earned his living by performing religious ceremonies in the local villages. The Brahmin owned a cow. He kept very good care of her and she gave him lots of milk.

One day a thief was passing the Brahmin's house, when he spotted the cow grazing in the small garden. He decided he would steal it later that night. There was a dark forest not far from the house, so he hid there and waited until dark.

Meanwhile, a terrible giant lived in the forest. He was planning to eat the Brahmin that very night! As the giant crept out of the forest, he bumped into the thief, who was also on his way to the Brahmin's house.

"Where are you going?" roared the giant.

"I'm going to the Brahmin's house to steal his cow," said the thief, trembling a little at the sight of the giant.

The giant grinned at the thief. This was his lucky night. After he had eaten the Brahmin, he would eat the thief and the cow. "Let's go together," he said. "While I eat the Brahmin, you can steal his cow."

The thief agreed, relieved that the giant hadn't eaten him!

By the time they reached the house, the Brahmin was fast asleep. The thief started to creep into the garden.

"What are you doing?" whispered the giant. "Let me eat the Brahmin first and then you can steal the cow."

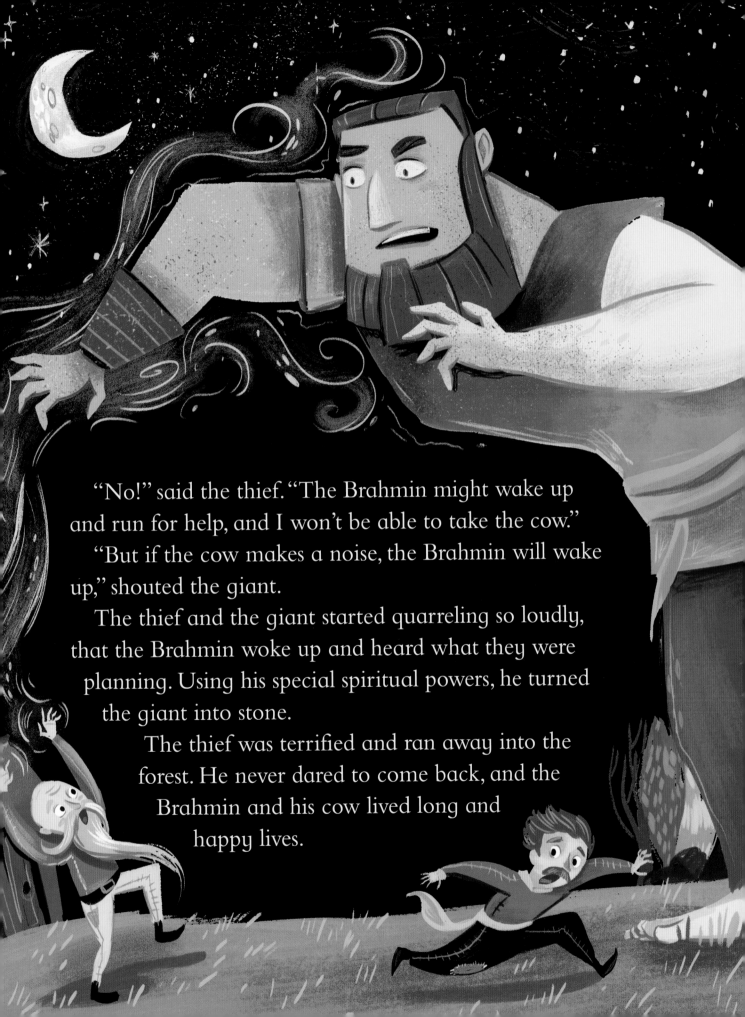

"No!" said the thief. "The Brahmin might wake up and run for help, and I won't be able to take the cow."

"But if the cow makes a noise, the Brahmin will wake up," shouted the giant.

The thief and the giant started quarreling so loudly, that the Brahmin woke up and heard what they were planning. Using his special spiritual powers, he turned the giant into stone.

The thief was terrified and ran away into the forest. He never dared to come back, and the Brahmin and his cow lived long and happy lives.

Just the Way You Are!

One day there was a knock on Frank the Rabbit's mossy front door. It was his best friend, James.

"It's my birthday and I'm having a party," said James. "I want to invite all my rabbit friends, and you're top of the list!"

Frank the Rabbit loved dancing. He danced in the street. He danced when he went shopping. He even danced in his sleep. But wherever he was dancing, it ended the same way. He always got overexcited, thumped his big feet on the ground, thumpity-thumpity-thumpity-thump, and made everything come crashing down around him. Disaster! People always got annoyed with Frank, even though he never meant to be naughty.

"James, you know what happens if I go to parties," Frank said, groaning. "I always end up breaking things with my big feet and upsetting everyone."

"You could never upset me," said James, putting his arm around Frank. "You're my best friend. Please come."

Frank looked at his smiling friend and had to say yes. So later that day, he arrived at the party feeling very nervous indeed.

"Definitely no dancing," he told his feet. "No tapping. And definitely no thumpity-thumpity-thumpity-thumping!"

At first, everything went well. Frank played hide-and-go-seek and ate three cupcakes. But then someone turned the music on, and the first song was FRANK'S FAVORITE. First, his big toe on one foot started tapping. Then all his toes. . .then both feet. And then—oh dear—Frank was leaping and hopping and bopping to the music. He spun and slid and whirled and twirled. He flung his arms and kicked up his legs. He forgot all about being careful. CRASH! The plates of party food flew through the air. He bounced into the air, spinning, and his ears got tangled up in the party decorations. They all came tumbling down around the other guests.

The song ended, and Frank looked around at the other guests. His heart sank.

"I've done it again," he said with a groan. "I'm so so sorry, James," he said.

James looked surprised. "What are you sorry for?" he asked.

"I've spoiled your party with my dancing," said Frank, and his ears drooped. But James gave him a big hug.

"You silly billy!" he said with a laugh. "You haven't spoiled my party! Everyone loved your dancing. Look!"

He pointed at the other guests. No one was looking cross or tidying up the mess. In fact, they were making it worse! They were tapping, thumping, and bopping to the music. Everyone was copying Frank's dance moves, and they all looked very happy.

A big smile spread across Frank's face.

"I thought I had to change to fit in with everyone else," he said.

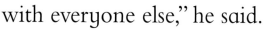

"I don't want you to change a single thing," said James. "You love dancing and it makes you happy, so it makes me happy too. You're my best friend—just the way you are!"

How the Leopard Got Its Spots

Long ago, Leopard lived on a sandy-yellow plain in Africa. Giraffes and zebras and deer lived there too. The animals were sandy-yellow all over, just like the plain itself. Leopard was sandy-yellow, too, which wasn't good for the rest of the animals because he could hide in the sandy-yellow grasses, then jump out and eat them.

After a while the other animals had had enough. They decided to move away from the sandy plain into the forest. In the forest, the sun shone through the trees, making stripy, spotty, and patchy shadows on the ground.

The animals hid themselves there, and while they hid, their skins changed color, becoming stripy, spotty, and patchy too.

Meanwhile, Leopard was hungry.

"Where has everyone gone?" he asked Baboon.

"To the forest," said Baboon carelessly, "to hide from you!"

Leopard decided to go to the forest to hunt for his dinner. But when he got there, all he could see were tree trunks. They were stripy, spotty, and patchy with shadows. He couldn't see the other animals, but he could smell them, so he knew they were there.

Meanwhile, the other animals could easily spot the sandy-yellow leopard in the forest, so they stayed hidden away.

Hungry and tired, Leopard lay down in a spotty shadow to rest. After a while, he noticed he wasn't sandy-yellow any more. He had small, dark spots on his skin just like the spotty shadow he was lying in.

"A-ha!" he thought. "Giraffe and Zebra and the other animals must have changed skin color too. But now my skin is no longer sandy-yellow, I can hide too. Then, when they come close, I can leap out and eat them up."

With that, the spotty leopard set off into the shadowy forest to eat, sleep, and NOT be spotted. And the other animals learned to hide from him as best they could, too!

The Sly Fox and the Little Red Hen

There was once a little red hen who lived all by herself in a house in the woods. Not far away, a sly fox lived in an underground burrow with his mother. The fox wanted to eat the little red hen for supper!

Every day, the little red hen left her house to collect sticks for her fire, but the fox never managed to catch her. She was far too clever for the fox and she knew all his tricks.

One morning, the sly fox picked up an old sack and set out to try and catch the little red hen.

"Mother," he shouted toward his burrow. "Put a pot of water on the fire to boil, for tonight we shall have the little red hen for our supper."

Then the fox hid behind a tree and waited until the little red hen left her house. As soon as she was out of sight, the sly fox sneaked into her house and hid behind the door.

A few minutes later, the little red hen returned. She closed the door and the cunning fox jumped out. The poor little red hen was so frightened that she dropped all her sticks and flew up to a high beam.

"You can't catch me now, Mr. Fox," she cried. "I won't come down."

"Ah," sighed the sly fox, grinning. "We'll soon see about that." And he started running around in a circle, chasing his tail.

Round and round he went. The poor little red hen watched him until she was so dizzy that she dropped off her perch. Quick as a flash, the sly fox grabbed her, threw her in his sack, and set off for home.

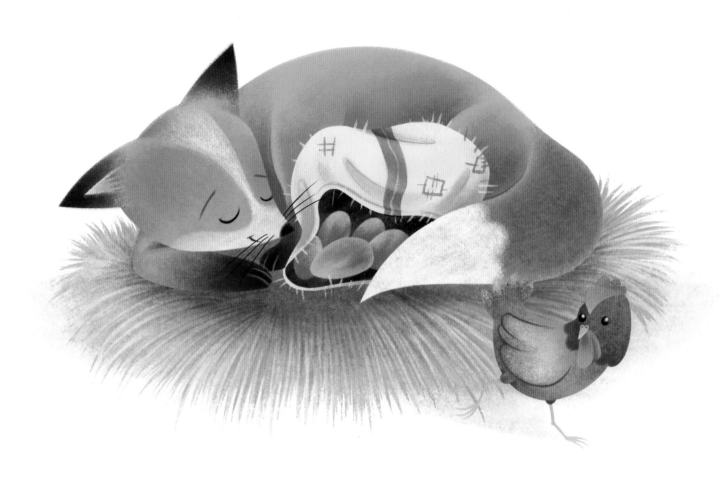

Before long, the sly fox sat down for a rest. As soon as the fox was asleep, the little red hen climbed out of the sack. Quickly, she collected some large stones and put them into the sack. Then she ran all the way home as fast as her little legs would carry her.

A while later, the sly fox woke up and set off for his burrow. The sack felt very heavy.

"The little red hen must be fatter than I thought," he said. "What a delicious meal she'll make!"

As soon as he got home, the fox shouted out to his mother, "Is the pot of water boiling? I have the little red hen at last! Lift the lid and let me drop her in."

His mother took the lid off the pot and the sly fox tipped the sack up and shook it. The heavy stones fell with a splash, right into the water.

And from that day on, the sly fox never tried to catch the little red hen ever again.

As for the little red hen, she lived safely and happily for the rest of her days.

Don't Be Scared

Dad put his arm around Little Cub. "I think the time's right for you to come out with me to explore tonight."

Little Cub peered at the evening sky. The sun was slipping down behind the trees. Shadows stretched across the plain.

As they set off, Little Cub shivered, and suddenly stopped.

"What's that high up there in that tree?" he asked. "There are two great big eyes watching me."

"Look closer, Little Cub. That thing up there is just old Owl. Did he give you a scare?" asked Dad.

"Dad," smiled Little Cub, "Owl won't give me a scare. He can't do that, as long as you're there."

Suddenly, Little Cub stopped. "What's that black shape hanging down from that tree? I felt it reaching out for me."

"Look closer, Little Cub. That thing up there is just old Snake. Did he give you a scare?" asked Dad.

"Dad," smiled Little Cub, "Snake won't give me a scare. He can't do that, as long as you're there."

Dad and Little Cub walked on. Suddenly, Little Cub stopped.

"What's that I can hear
behind that tree? There's a
   huge black shadow following us."

   "Look closer, Little Cub. That thing
back there is just old Elephant. Did he give
you a scare?" asked Dad.

   "Dad," smiled Little Cub, "Elephant won't give me a scare.
He can't do that, as long as you're there."

   Dad and Little Cub walked on. Suddenly, Dad stopped.

   "What's that?" he asked.

   "Hooooo, hooooo! Sssss, Sssss! Terummmp, terummmp!"

   The animals jumped out at Dad. Dad jumped!

   "Don't be scared," laughed Little Cub.

   The animals laughed. "Sorry, Lion! Did we give you a
fright?" they asked.

   "No!" said Dad, smiling. "You couldn't give me a scare.
Not as long as Little Cub is there."

   Then, side by side, Little Cub and Dad headed for home.

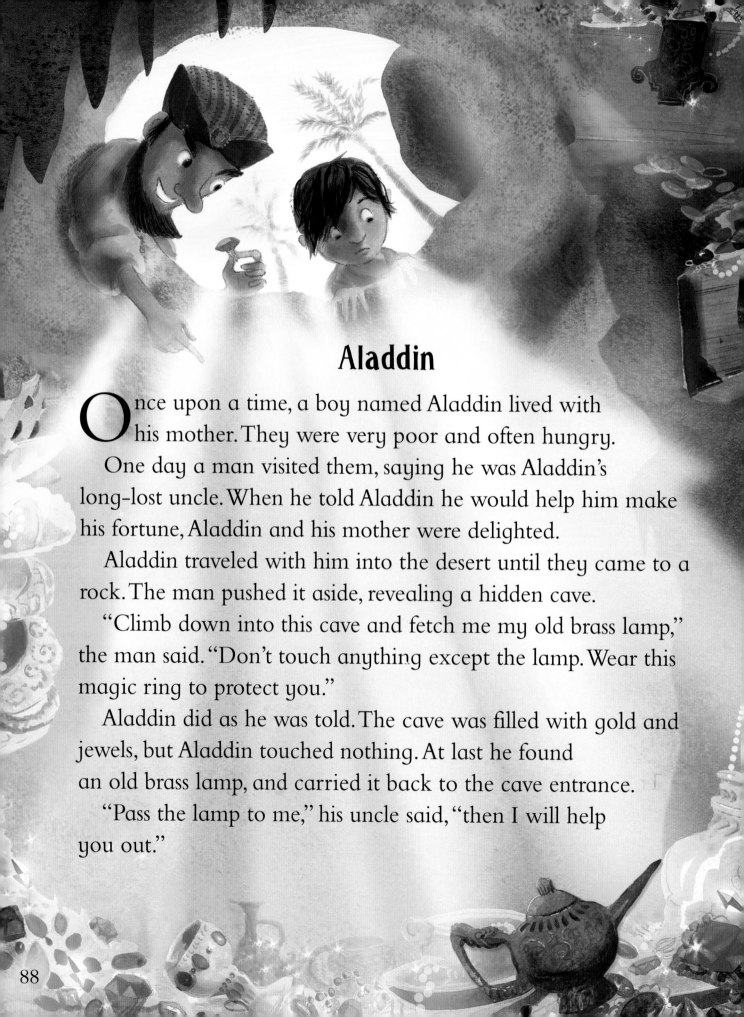

Aladdin

Once upon a time, a boy named Aladdin lived with
his mother. They were very poor and often hungry.

One day a man visited them, saying he was Aladdin's
long-lost uncle. When he told Aladdin he would help him make
his fortune, Aladdin and his mother were delighted.

Aladdin traveled with him into the desert until they came to a
rock. The man pushed it aside, revealing a hidden cave.

"Climb down into this cave and fetch me my old brass lamp,"
the man said. "Don't touch anything except the lamp. Wear this
magic ring to protect you."

Aladdin did as he was told. The cave was filled with gold and
jewels, but Aladdin touched nothing. At last he found
an old brass lamp, and carried it back to the cave entrance.

"Pass the lamp to me," his uncle said, "then I will help
you out."

But Aladdin wanted to be let out first, before he gave his uncle the lamp. This made his uncle angry.

"Fool!" the man roared, and he rolled the rock back over the cave, trapping Aladdin inside.

"Uncle! Let me out!" Aladdin cried.

"I'm not your uncle," said the man. "I'm a sorcerer! Stay there for good if you won't give me the lamp."

As Aladdin wrung his hands in despair, he rubbed the magic ring on his finger.

Suddenly, a genie sprang out and asked: "What do you require, master?"

Astonished, Aladdin told the genie to take him home. In a flash, Aladdin was outside his mother's house.

Still poor and hungry, Aladdin polished the old lamp, hoping to sell it to get money for food. But as he rubbed the lamp clean, another genie jumped out.

This time, Aladdin asked for food and money so that he and his mother could live in comfort.

Life went on happily until, one day, Aladdin fell hopelessly in love with the emperor's beautiful daughter. But how could he, Aladdin, marry a princess? Suddenly, he had an idea … he asked the genie of the lamp for gifts to give to the princess.

When the princess thanked Aladdin for the gifts, she fell in love with him. They were soon married, and Aladdin asked the genie to build them a beautiful palace.

Hearing that a wealthy stranger had married the princess, the wicked sorcerer guessed that Aladdin must have escaped with the lamp.

One day, when Aladdin was out, the sorcerer disguised himself as a poor tradesman. He stood outside the palace calling out, "New lamps for old! New lamps for old!"

Aladdin's wife gave her husband's old brass lamp to the sorcerer, who snatched it away and rubbed the lamp. He commanded the genie to carry the palace and the princess far away.

"Oh, no!" cried Aladdin, when he discovered his wife and home gone.

Quickly, he rubbed the magic ring to make the genie appear.

"Please bring back my wife and palace!" Aladdin pleaded.

"Sorry, master, I can't!" said the genie. "I am less powerful than the genie of the lamp."

"Then take me to her and I'll win her back!" Aladdin cried.

At once, he found himself in a strange city, but outside his own palace. Through a window he saw his wife crying, and the sorcerer sleeping. Aladdin crept into the palace. He grabbed the magic lamp and rubbed it.

"What do you require, master?" asked the genie.

"Take us straight back home," Aladdin said, "and shut this wicked sorcerer in the cave for a thousand years!"

In a moment, the palace was back where it belonged. With the sorcerer gone, Aladdin and the princess were safe, and they never needed to call on the genie again.

Kiera the Kite

It was a dark and stormy night, and Kiera the kite was one of the few creatures who dared to go out. She had a chick to feed and had left her mountaintop nest to hunt.

At last Kiera managed to snare a juicy mouse and set off for home. She flapped her powerful wings and battled against the wind. The wind was so strong that she couldn't fly very fast. It was almost dawn when she finally spotted her nest. She swooped down in triumph, and then shuddered to a halt.

"Squawk!" she cried. Her nest was empty! Where was her baby? Kiera hopped around in alarm. She didn't know what to do. Then she had an idea. She flapped her wings and soared high into the sky. Hovering above the ground, she scanned the area with sharp eyes. Almost immediately she spotted a movement far below and swooped down. Kiera screeched with joy. There was her little chick, sitting safely on a rocky ledge.

"I'm okay," squeaked the little chick. "I jumped out of the nest because it was swaying in the wind."

"I think it's time to teach you how to fly," smiled Kiera.

A New Pool for Otter

Otter had lived in the animal sanctuary for as long as he could remember. Then, one day, his keeper lifted him out of his pen and placed him in a crate. Otter was so scared that he couldn't move. He curled into a ball and shook with fright as the lid closed and everything went dark.

"What's happening?" he wondered.

Otter felt himself being carried along and put down. Then a door slammed, and an engine roared into life. The engine purred as Otter bumped gently around in his crate. Finally the engine stopped and the door was opened. Otter's crate was lifted out and placed on to the ground. Sunlight flooded in as the lid opened. Otter blinked and sniffed the air. He looked around before creeping out. Suddenly, he was bursting with happiness. There in front of him was a woodland pool, twinkling in the sun.

"Welcome home!" smiled his keeper. SPLASH! Otter dived into the crystal-clear water and darted after the fish. He was free …

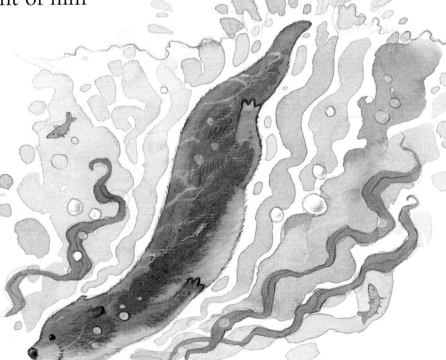

The Clever Tailor

A long time ago, there lived a very proud princess. Her parents were eager for her to find a husband, but the princess said that she would only marry someone who was clever enough to answer one of her questions. She had many suitors, but none of them ever got the correct answer.

One day, a young tailor came to the palace to make a cloak for the king. When he heard about the princess, he decided to try his luck.

The princess was sure the tailor wouldn't guess the answer to her question.

"I have two different kinds of hair on my head. What color are they?" she asked.

The tailor thought for a while and then he said, "You have one silver and one golden hair on your head."

The princess gasped, for the tailor had guessed correctly. Then she said, "You must do something else for me first, to prove you are really worthy of me."

The tailor agreed.

"You must spend the night in the stable with a bear," said the princess. "If you are still alive in the morning, I will marry you."

The princess, thinking she would soon be rid of the tailor, went off happily to her room.

In the stable, the tailor calmly took out a little fiddle and started to play a jolly tune on it. When the bear heard the music, he could not help dancing.

"Oh, I wish I could play the fiddle," the bear growled. "Then I could dance whenever I wanted to."

"Well, I could teach you," said the tailor. "But your claws are far too long; you need to file them down first."

The bear looked all around the stable until he found a file. The tailor knew that it would take hours for the bear to file down his long, sharp claws, so he lay down and fell fast asleep.

When the princess went down to the stables in the morning, she was shocked to see the clever tailor giving the bear a fiddle lesson. She knew she couldn't break her promise to the tailor again, so the next day she married him. And because the tailor was clever and funny, the princess soon grew to love him. She had finally met someone as smart as herself, and the pair lived happily ever after.

Mabel Gets Lost

One sunny day, Mrs. Duck took her ducklings for a swim. "Whatever you do, stay close, and don't wander off," she warned her brood.

But Mabel, the smallest duckling, wasn't listening. She was too busy chasing butterflies. Mabel waddled along behind a colorful butterfly until it disappeared across the river. Then she looked around. She had wandered a long way from home, and had never seen this part of the river before. But Mabel didn't mind. There were lots of interesting things to see. She watched a blue kingfisher diving for fish. Then she saw some otters playing on the bank. Above, a flock of swans soared across the sky.

"Quack, quack!" she cried. "This is an exciting place!"

She called out to the otters, but they were too busy messing around to hear her. Suddenly, Mabel began to miss her mom and her brothers and sisters.

"I'd better go home," she quacked. But when she looked around, Mabel didn't know which way to go.

"Oh, no," she wailed. "I'm lost." And she sat down beside the river to cry. She had been crying for a few minutes when the water in front her began to ripple. Then two bulging eyes, followed by a green head, popped up. It was her friend Herbert the frog. Mabel gulped and tried to wipe away her tears.

"What's wrong?" Herbert asked kindly.

"I'm lost," wept Mabel. "And I miss my mom."

"Don't worry," croaked Herbert. "Jump into the river and swim behind me. I'll show you the way home."

So Mabel followed Herbert downstream until they bumped into Mrs. Duck and the other ducklings.

"Hooray! I'm home at last!" quacked Mabel, leaping out of the water and rushing to her mom's side.

Mrs. Duck was so pleased to see her that she forgot to be angry.

"I'll stay close to you from now on," quacked Mabel.

Granny's Little Elephant

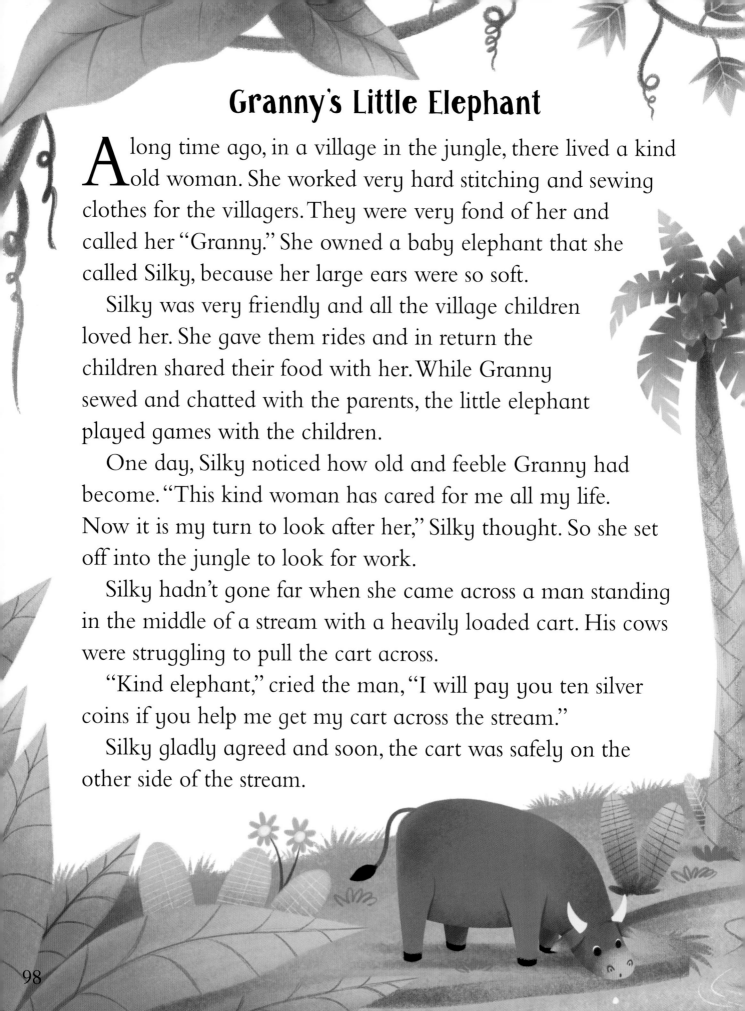

A long time ago, in a village in the jungle, there lived a kind old woman. She worked very hard stitching and sewing clothes for the villagers. They were very fond of her and called her "Granny." She owned a baby elephant that she called Silky, because her large ears were so soft.

Silky was very friendly and all the village children loved her. She gave them rides and in return the children shared their food with her. While Granny sewed and chatted with the parents, the little elephant played games with the children.

One day, Silky noticed how old and feeble Granny had become. "This kind woman has cared for me all my life. Now it is my turn to look after her," Silky thought. So she set off into the jungle to look for work.

Silky hadn't gone far when she came across a man standing in the middle of a stream with a heavily loaded cart. His cows were struggling to pull the cart across.

"Kind elephant," cried the man, "I will pay you ten silver coins if you help me get my cart across the stream."

Silky gladly agreed and soon, the cart was safely on the other side of the stream.

"Thank you," said the man. He handed Silky five coins, then started to guide his cows down the path through the jungle.

"Stop!" shouted Silky. "You've only given me half the money you promised."

But the man ignored Silky and carried on down the path.

Silky was very upset with the man's dishonesty, so she ran round the cart and stopped in the middle of the track.

The man pushed and pushed, but he could not budge Silky. Finally, he gave up and handed over the rest of the money.

Silky rushed home to give Granny her first hard-earned wages. Granny hugged Silky tightly—she had been getting worried. Then Silky told her the whole story. Granny was so proud of her elephant.

"Now you don't have to work so hard," said Silky. "I'll look after you."

Mowgli's Brothers

As the sun set over the jungle, the Wolf family stirred in their cave. Father Wolf prepared to go hunting, while Mother Wolf watched over her four playful cubs.

As Father Wolf left the cave, he heard a terrifying roar. It was Shere Khan the tiger, the most feared animal in the whole of the jungle. Suddenly, the bushes rustled and Father Wolf prepared to pounce. But it wasn't Shere Khan. It was a naked baby.

"A man cub!" gasped Father Wolf.

"Quick, bring him into the cave!" cried Mother Wolf. The baby snuggled up against Mother Wolf, just as Shere Khan appeared at the cave entrance.

"Give me the man cub," roared the huge tiger. "I've hunted him through the jungle and he's mine."

The wolves knew Shere Khan was too big to get into the cave so they stood their ground.

"No!" Mother Wolf shouted. "He will not be killed. We will bring him up with our cubs. Now go!"

The cowardly tiger knew he was no match for all the wolves working together. Slinking off back into the jungle, he cried, "We will see what the Pack Council has to say about you adopting a man cub."

"We will keep him," Mother Wolf declared. "And we will call him Mowgli."

At the next full moon, the Pack Council met to decide whether Mowgli could stay. Shere Khan arrived to try and persuade the wolves to hand over the man cub. Some of the younger wolves in the pack agreed with him, but Akela, the leader of the pack, spoke out.

"You all know the rules. If two people, other than his parents, can speak in favor of him, Mowgli can stay. Who speaks for this cub?" he cried.

"I speak for the man cub," said a loud voice. "I myself will watch out for him."

It was Baloo, the brown bear whose job it was to teach the wolf cubs the Law of the Jungle.

"Me too!" purred the soft voice of Bagheera, the black panther. Everyone knew the wise panther and all respected him.

"It's settled them," said Akela. "The man cub can stay. He may be a help to us one day."

Many years passed and Mowgli grew big and strong. He learned all about the jungle, and he ran and hunted with the pack. Sometimes Mowgli would creep down to the village and watch the people. He knew they were his kind, but he was happy with his wolf family and animal friends.

Shere Khan was biding his time. Bagheera knew that he would try and kill Mowgli one day.

And that day came soon enough, when Akela was too old and feeble to run the pack and protect Mowgli any more. The younger wolves wanted to hand Mowgli over to the ferocious tiger and they turned against Akela.

"Mowgli, run to the village," hissed Bagheera, "and fetch the Red Flower."

Bagheera was referring to fire. All the animals were scared of man's fire.

Mowgli returned to the pack waving a burning branch. They cowered in fear.

"If you let Akela go, I will go to the village and live among people."

Mowgli thrust the fire toward Shere Khan. "As for you,"
he shouted, "next time I see you, there will be trouble."
The cowardly tiger scampered away in fright.
With tears in his eyes, Mowgli said farewell to his wolf family.
"We will miss you," cried Mother Wolf.
"I'll visit," said Mowgli, before setting off to his new life.

The Mouse and the Weasel

One day, a hungry mouse came across a basket of grain in a barn. There was a lid on the basket, and the farmer had put a brick on top to keep out mice and rats, but the little mouse was starving and determined to get to the grain.

The mouse ran around and around and up and down the basket until he found a narrow space between the strips of wood. Normally the mouse would never have been able to squeeze through such a tiny hole, but he was so thin by now that he just managed to wriggle his way into the basket.

The mouse was so hungry that he ate, and ate, and ate. And then he ate some more. At last he felt satisfied and burrowed his way back through the grain, until he found the space in the basket again.

But the hole suddenly looked very, very small—and the mouse was feeling very, very fat! In fact, his stomach was three times as big as it had been when he had squeezed his way in.

The mouse pushed his head through the hole and wriggled. It was no use. He couldn't get through. So he tried to pull his head back in again, only to find that he was completely stuck. He couldn't move backward or forward.

Just then, a weasel passed by. He saw the mouse's head sticking out of the basket and guessed what had happened.

"I know what you've been doing," laughed Weasel. "You've been stuffing yourself with food and now you are stuck. It's your own fault. I don't have any sympathy for you, I'm afraid! You will just have to wait there without eating until you are thin enough to get out again."

And that's exactly what the greedy little mouse had to do.

And the moral of the story is: greed often leads to misfortune.

The Woodpecker, the Tortoise, and the Deer

Once upon a time, three best friends, a woodpecker, a tortoise, and a deer, lived in a forest near a lake. One night, the deer got caught in a hunter's net.

"Help, dear friends!" she cried. "Come quickly, I'm trapped!"

At once, the woodpecker and the tortoise came to see what had happened.

"Tortoise, gnaw through the ropes as quickly as you can," said the woodpecker. "I'll find the hunter and keep him away."

The tortoise started biting the ropes and the woodpecker flew off to the hunter's hideout. When the hunter opened the door to go and check on his trap, the woodpecker pecked him and flapped his wings in his face. Surprised, the hunter rushed back inside and slammed the door shut.

"What am I going to do?" the hunter wondered. Gathering his courage, and a sack, he opened the door again. "If you attack me again," he shouted, "I'll catch you!" And he flapped the sack until the woodpecker flew away.

"Hurry, Tortoise!" called the woodpecker. "The hunter is on his way."

By the time the hunter arrived, the tortoise had gnawed away most of the rope. The deer broke the last strand with her hoof and ran into the forest. The poor tortoise was very tired from chewing through the net, and couldn't run away. The hunter picked him up and put him in his sack, then he tied the sack to a tree.

When the deer saw that her friend was in trouble, she let the hunter see her. The hunter rushed after the deer. Soon, he was lost in the forest. Meanwhile, the clever deer had found another way back to the lake. Using her sharp horns, she ripped the sack open, and freed the tortoise.

"We must hide until the hunter has gone for good," said the deer.

The hunter finally found his way out of the woods. He was annoyed that he had lost the deer. "At least I still have the tortoise," he sighed to himself. But when he untied the sack, he saw that the tortoise had escaped. "I'm never hunting again," he shouted angrily, and stomped all the way home.

As for the three best friends, they all lived peacefully ever after.

A Golden Touch

There was once a king who wished that everything he touched would turn to gold.

His wish was granted by a passing fairy, and he ran around his palace turning all his belongings into gold. Vases, statues, plates, and even cushions were turned to gold as soon as he touched them.

"I will be so rich," he thought.

Before long, the king started to feel hungry. "Bring me some fruit," he ordered his servant. But when the king picked up an apple, it turned to gold before it had even reached his lips.

The king began to feel very sad, but when his wife tried to comfort him with a hug, even she turned to gold.

"I never want to see gold again," sobbed the king and he wished with all his heart for things to be back to normal.

Luckily, the fairy, who had been watching all along, took pity on him. Everything changed back to the way it had been before. The king had learned his lesson and he knew that there were many ordinary things more valuable than gold.

King Canute and the Ocean

King Canute was a powerful king. His courtiers were always flattering him so that they could stay in his favor.

One day, the king's courtiers persuaded him that he was so powerful that he would be able to stop the tide coming in.

King Canute, believing their flattery, went down to the beach and sat on his throne waiting for the tide to turn so that he could command it to stop.

"I command you to stop," he bellowed as the sea came in. But the tide did not stop. King Canute sat steadfast on his throne. "I command you to stop," he bellowed again, but still the sea paid no heed.

The courtiers backed away as the sea came closer, but still the king would not leave his throne. When the sea began to cover the king's feet, he realized that he was not as powerful as he'd thought. He ruled more wisely from then on.

Jasper the Dancing Zebra!

Most zebras are happy galloping or grazing. But not Jasper. He loved to dance!

He tapped his hooves all through breakfast. He hip-hopped across the hills until lunchtime. He shimmied his way through the searing heat of the afternoon.

And by the light of the moon, he twirled until his legs were so tired that finally, he had to stop!

Day after day, Jasper danced. The grassy plains echoed with the sound of his clickety-clackety hooves and his happy braying as he leapt and pirouetted.

The trouble was Jasper was so busy dancing, that he forgot to do his chores.

"Jasper never helps gather the leaves and fruit," moaned the other zebras.

"But he always enjoys eating them!" cried Florence.

"It's not fair! We should teach him a lesson," said Zachary.

That evening as Jasper returned home for supper, he was surprised to see the other zebras standing quietly. There were no leaves or fruits on the ground.

"Where's supper?" asked Jasper.

"We've already eaten," replied Florence. "You'll have to get your own."

The same thing happened the next few nights.

By the fourth evening, Jasper was feeling very unhappy. He didn't tap his hooves or sway. Tears trickled down his face.

After a while Florence came over. "We didn't mean to upset you, but we wanted to teach you a lesson," she said gently.

Jasper drooped his head. "I'm sorry. I promise I will help with the chores from now on," he whispered.

"And we really do love your dancing," said Zachary, "but just not ALL the time!"

Jasper smiled shyly at his friends. "I'll do extra jobs tomorrow," he said. "But let me do a special dance for you now, to show you how sorry I am!"

And everyone laughed, as Jasper leaped and swirled under the light of the moon.

The Little Lamb

One sunny morning, Little Lamb decided to go and visit his grandma who lived across the meadow, over the stream, and on the other side of the forest.

As he skipped across the meadow, Little Lamb saw Jackal, hiding in the long grass.

Jackal was feeling hungry. He jumped up and growled, "Little Lamb, I'm going to eat you!"

But Little Lamb wasn't afraid.

"I'm off to visit Granny, where I shall get fatter, and then you can eat me!" he laughed.

Jackal thought this sounded like a good plan, so he let the lamb pass.

Little Lamb skipped away. When he reached the stream, a huge vulture swept down and eyed the lamb hungrily.

"Little Lamb, I'm going to eat you!" Vulture screeched.

Little Lamb looked up at Vulture and sang in a merry little voice, "I'm off to visit Granny, where I shall get fatter, and then you can eat me!"

Vulture thought this sounded like a good plan, so he let the lamb pass.

Little Lamb crossed the stream and came to the forest. A fearsome tiger crept out of the trees.

"Little Lamb, I'm going to eat you!" growled Tiger.

Little Lamb laughed and sang, "I'm off to visit Granny, where I shall get fatter, and then you can eat me!"

Tiger thought this sounded like a good plan, so he let the lamb pass.

Granny was happy to see Little Lamb.

"Granny, I've promised to get fatter," said Little Lamb, "and I should keep my promise, so please put me in your grain bin."

Granny lifted Little Lamb into the grain bin. There he stayed for seven days. He ate and ate and ate, until he was so fat that Granny said he had kept his promise, and the other animals would want to eat him.

But Little Lamb had a clever plan to get home.

Little Lamb climbed inside a large drum and asked his granny to close the lid. Then he rolled out of her house and through the woods.

He passed Tiger in the forest, who growled, "Rolling drum, have you seen Little Lamb?"

Curled up safe and warm inside the drum, Little Lamb called out, "He fell in the fire and is all gone!" And off he trundled.

Vulture swooped down as Little Lamb floated across the stream. "Rolling drum, have you seen Little Lamb?"

"He fell in the fire and is all gone!" said Little Lamb, and rolled on.

Little Lamb was halfway across the meadow, when Jackal jumped in front of the drum.

"Rolling drum, have you seen Little Lamb?" he barked.

Trying not to laugh, Little Lamb replied, "He fell in the fire and is all gone!"

But Jackal recognized Little Lamb's voice. He pounced on the drum … but it rolled away from under him. The drum bowled faster and faster, and didn't stop until Little Lamb was safely home.

I Want to be a Scary Monster!

Pog was a little purple monster with boggly eyes, two horns, and two zig-zaggy wings. For such a small creature, Pog was incredibly LOUD!

Pog liked to stomp and crash and bang around the house at night when the children were sleeping, shouting "ARRRGH!" and bellowing "BOO!"

But no one was ever frightened!

If the children woke up they would just mumble, "Oh, it's only Pog", and go back to sleep, and the other monsters would laugh.

At first, Pog didn't really mind that no one screamed when they saw him. But secretly, he longed to be big and scary, like a real monster. After all, monsters weren't supposed to make people laugh!

So one night, when everything in the house was quiet, Pog crept out from his hiding place. He didn't stomp his paws. He didn't roar "BOO!" at the top of his booming voice.

Slowly Pog slithered across the floor until he was crouching right behind one of his monster friends. Silently, he stood up and flapped his wings to cast a huge frightening shadow on the wall.

"Oh, hello Pog, it's only you!" giggled his friend. "I'd recognize those zig-zaggy wings anywhere!"

"I just want to make someone scream!" Pog sobbed.

"Don't cry … ARRRGH! What's that?" screamed the other monster, jumping in fright.

Still sniffling, Pog turned to see what had frightened his friend.

"ARRRGH!" screamed Pog. "Yuck, it's a spider. SCARY!"

Pog looked at his friend. He grinned and suddenly they were both roaring with laughter.

"Oh, Pog! Look at us, scared of a little spider!" giggled the other monster. "You're so funny, you don't have to be scary. We all love you as you are."

Pog wiped away his tears and smiled shyly at his friend.

"BOO!" he shouted at the top of his voice. "It's only me!"

And all the other monsters laughed.

The Man Who Never Lied

Once upon a time there lived a wise man named Mamad. He never told lies. He was famous throughout the land for his wisdom and honesty.

The king had heard about Mamad. He decided to test the wise man's honesty for himself. So one morning, as he got ready to go hunting, he called the wise man to his side. With his left foot on the horse's stirrup, the king turned to Mamad.

"Go to my summer palace and tell the queen I will be with her for lunch. Tell her to prepare a big feast. You will then have lunch with me."

Mamad bowed to the king and set off to the palace. When he was out of sight, the king turned to his men and laughed.

"We won't go hunting and now Mamad will lie to the queen," he cried.

At the palace, Mamad spoke to the queen.

"Maybe you should prepare a big feast for lunch tomorrow, and maybe you shouldn't," said Mamad. "Maybe the king will come by noon, and maybe he won't."

"Tell me, will he come, or won't he?" asked the queen.

"I don't know whether he put his right foot on the other stirrup, or he put his left foot back on the ground after I left," replied Mamad.

Everybody waited for the king. He didn't arrive until the next day.

"The wise Mamad, who never lies, lied to you yesterday," boasted the king to the queen.

But the queen told him Mamad's exact words. The king realized that he couldn't fool Mamad. Indeed, a wise man never lies; he says only that which he sees with his own eyes.

Alex and the Egyptian Magic

So far, Alex wasn't enjoying Egypt very much. "You can write about the pyramids in your school journal," said his mom. But Alex didn't think the pyramids or the guide were very interesting.

"This pyramid was built as a tomb for a mummified Egyptian pharaoh king," the guide explained. "A special ancient magic keeps his tomb hidden, even though hundreds of people have looked for his treasure."

"I don't believe that," said Alex. Just then he spotted a tiny door in the side of the pyramid. While his parents weren't looking, he opened the door and crept inside. He found a long tunnel with hieroglyphics on the wall. Alex's heart thumped with excitement. At last something fun was happening!

He crawled along the tunnel until it opened out into a big chamber lit with flaming torches. He saw a mummy wrapped in white bandages, surrounded by glittering treasures. Golden goblets, necklaces, bowls, and statues sparkled with rubies and emeralds.

"I've found the mummy's treasure!" Alex exclaimed. But as soon as his finger touched a golden lamp, WHOOSH! Something yanked him out of the chamber and back to his parents and the tour guide.

Alex looked around in confusion. The little door had disappeared. "Are you all right?" asked his mom.

Alex tried to explain, but to his surprise he said, "Fine thanks." Something was stopping him from talking about the chamber! He looked at the guide, who simply winked.

"As I said," the guide went on, "the ancient magic won't let anyone reveal the king's tomb."

Alex smiled. At least now he had something interesting to write about in his school journal!

Seven Ravens

Once there lived a man and a woman who had seven sons but longed for a daughter. When their eighth child was a girl, they were very happy. At last their wish had come true.

The beautiful baby girl was a thirsty little thing, so the seven sons were sent out to the well to fetch water.

"Take this silver cup and fill it for the baby," said their mother. But the silver cup fell into the well with a splash! The boys were too frightened to go home.

When they didn't return, their father cursed them. "May those lazy good-for-nothing boys become ravens!" he shouted. As soon as the words left his mouth, he saw seven ravens flying off into the distance. Although he regretted his words, it was too late to undo his curse.

When the little girl grew older, her sad mother told her all about her seven lost brothers. The brave girl vowed to find them and bring them home.

She set off, taking her mother's ring as a keepsake, and searched the world over.

"Where are my seven brothers?" she called up to the heavens. The stars could see that the poor girl was in despair and took pity on her. They sent down a magical key and, as the girl picked it up, she heard these words:

"Follow our light to a mountain of glass,
You'll find your raven brothers at last."

After walking for many days, the young girl finally reached the glass mountain. Using the key she entered a crystal cave and, although nobody was there, she noticed seven little plates and cups laid out with food and drink ready for their return.

Being very hungry, she took a bite from each plate and a sip from each cup. Her ring fell into the last cup but, before she could pick it up again, she heard the swish of wings. She hid behind a door and watched seven ravens swoop down.

Each raven noticed that some of their food and drink was missing. Then the last raven found the ring in his cup and recognized it as his mother's.

"If only our little sister would come to find us," he exclaimed, "for then we could return home with her."

On hearing this, their brave little sister cried out with joy. As soon as they saw her, the ravens turned back into men.

Reunited at long last, they returned home and lived happily ever after.

The Stubborn Little Pig

Joe's best friend wasn't another boy or girl. It wasn't a dog or a cat. It was a pig!

"A pig can't be a real friend," said the grown-ups. But Joe didn't agree.

"He's the best pig in the world," Joe said.

They did everything together. They splashed in streams. They chased each other around meadows. And whenever Joe needed to share a secret or try out a new joke, his friend was always there to listen. There was just one problem. The little pig was very, very stubborn. If he didn't want to do something, no one could make him do it.

"You can't always have your own way, you know," said Joe. "Sometimes you have to let someone else have a turn."

But the little pig just gazed at him until Joe gave in and did what the little pig wanted.

One morning Joe had a bright idea.

"I know how to stop my little pig from being so stubborn," he exclaimed. "He needs to go to school!"

"But how will school help?" asked Dad, while they all ate breakfast.

"Everyone has to do what the teachers say; otherwise they'll get told off," Joe explained. "I bet they'll be able to help him get rid of his stubbornness."

So Joe put his little pig friend on a lead and they set off together. But when they came to the road opposite the school, the little pig stopped.

"Oh no," groaned Joe. "He doesn't want to cross the road."

A policeman was passing by, and he stopped to help.

"Hello, young man," he said. "What seems to be the problem?"

"My pig won't cross the road," said Joe. "We're going to be late for school!"

The policeman frowned at the pig. "Now then, young pig, you must cross this road. I'm a policeman, so you must do what I say."

The policeman stared at the pig, and the pig stared at the policeman. Then the little pig sat down on the pavement and shook his little head.

"The traffic is waiting for you," said the policeman. "You have to cross the road."

It was no use. The little pig didn't move one bit. The cars were hooting and a traffic jam was forming. Even worse than that, it was almost time for school to start. Joe would be in big trouble if he was late. He looked across the road and saw lots of children hurrying into the school with their friends.

Then, suddenly, Joe had an idea. He kneeled down and whispered something into the pig's ear. The little pig looked at him and gave a little snort. Then it stood up and trotted across the road. When they reached the other side, the policeman hurried after them.

"What did you say?" he asked.

Joe grinned. "I told him that he is my best friend and I need him to be at school with me," he said.

Everyone likes to be needed—even stubborn little pigs!

X Marks the Spot

Jim's best friend Aaron was a lot of fun, but there was just one problem. He was very, very forgetful.

One day they were playing in Aaron's yard when they found a treasure map.

"X marks the spot!" Jim exclaimed. "Let's follow the map and find the treasure."

They packed binoculars, a flashlight, and a compass, and set off to follow the map. First, it led them to the cobwebby garden shed. Aaron's pet cat peeped out of a box in the corner, but there was no treasure.

"Where is it?" asked Aaron.

"We need to find the X," said Jim. "X marks the spot."

"Oh, yes, I forgot," said Aaron.

Next, the map pointed Jim, Aaron, and the cat to the birdbath on the lawn. A bird was splashing around in it, but there was no treasure.

"Where is it?" asked Aaron.

"X marks the spot, remember?" said Jim.

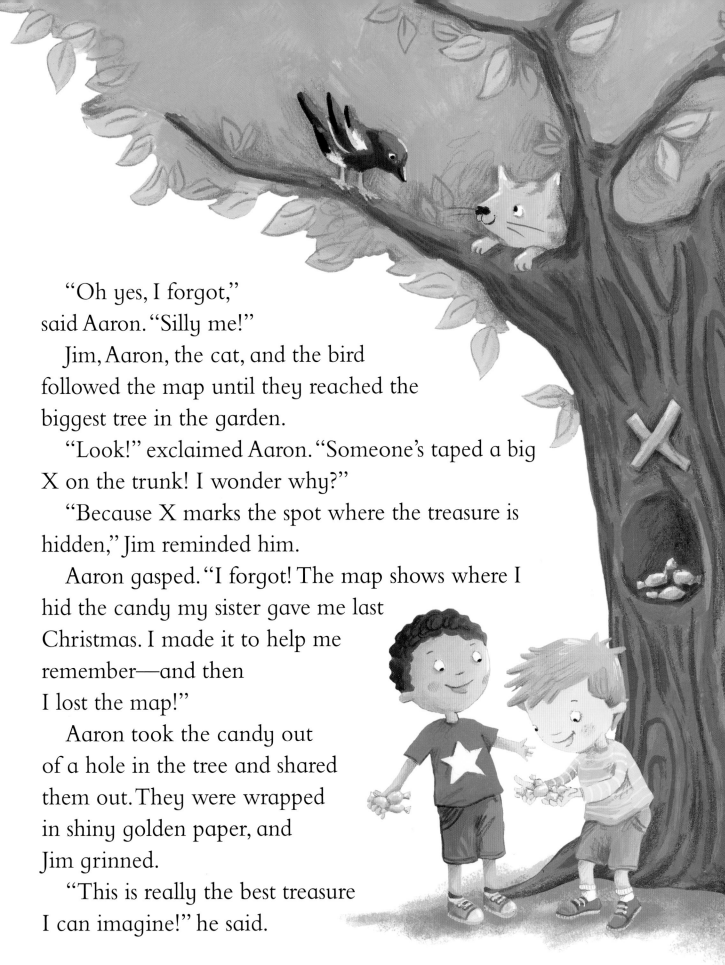

"Oh yes, I forgot,"
said Aaron. "Silly me!"

Jim, Aaron, the cat, and the bird
followed the map until they reached the
biggest tree in the garden.

"Look!" exclaimed Aaron. "Someone's taped a big
X on the trunk! I wonder why?"

"Because X marks the spot where the treasure is
hidden," Jim reminded him.

Aaron gasped. "I forgot! The map shows where I
hid the candy my sister gave me last
Christmas. I made it to help me
remember—and then
I lost the map!"

Aaron took the candy out
of a hole in the tree and shared
them out. They were wrapped
in shiny golden paper, and
Jim grinned.

"This is really the best treasure
I can imagine!" he said.

The Tin Soldier

Once there was a little boy who lived in a townhouse at the end of a leafy avenue. It was a very happy home.

On the boy's birthday there were balloons, a magnificent cake, and a small pile of colorfully wrapped presents. The boy undid the ribbon and pulled back the paper on the first package, his eyes glittering with anticipation.

"Tin soldiers!" cried the boy in excitement, as he opened his present. "Thank you, Mom and Dad. I love them!"

He lined them up along his playroom floor. When he got to the last soldier in the box, he paused.

"Oh!" he said. "This soldier has only one leg."

The soldiers had been cast from some old tin spoons and there hadn't been quite enough metal to finish the last man. Despite missing a leg, the tin soldier stood upright and steady.

"This one must go on parade, too," decided the boy. "He is just as smart and brave as the others."

The boy spent the rest of his birthday evening playing with his new toys. At the other end of the playroom there was a fine wooden castle.

When the boy carried the tin soldier with one leg past the toy castle, something caught the soldier's eye. There, in the doorway, was a beautiful paper doll ballerina. She stood on one leg, with her other leg pointed out behind her.

"She stands on one leg, just as I do," marveled the soldier. "What a wonderful wife she would make!"

Soon the boy left the room to go to bed. The tin soldier hid behind a box on the windowsill. From his hiding place, he gazed at the ballerina all night. In her castle, the ballerina was frozen too, fixed in her pose. The soldier and the dancer stared into each other's eyes all night long, not turning away for a moment.

When morning came, a maid came in to tidy the room. As she opened the window, she accidentally knocked the tin soldier over the ledge.

Down, down, down, the soldier fell, dropping at last into a drain in the street below.

"Stand tall, soldier! Meet your fate with courage!" he cried, as he was washed through dark pipes and out into a river.

As the tin soldier sank down into the murky waters of the river, he thought of the delicate ballerina to give him courage. Suddenly, everything went dark. The soldier had been swallowed by a big silver fish.

The fish twisted and turned in the water. But just when the soldier was certain that he would be crushed to death, the creature became still. The soldier stayed still, as light burst into the darkness. The fish had been caught and cut open and was lying in a kitchen, ready to be cooked.

"Oh, good heavens!" cried a voice. "Our lost soldier!"

By a stroke of good luck, the soldier had come back to the house of the little boy. The cook washed him and gave him to the maid to put back in the boy's playroom.

The soldier's heart burst with joy. He was near to his beloved ballerina once again.

The next day, however, as the boy played, he accidentally knocked the tin soldier into the fire.

"No!" cried the boy. But it was too late. The tin soldier had already started to melt away.

Suddenly, a gust of wind curled in through the open window, lifting the ballerina off her feet. She twirled once before disappearing in the flames beside the soldier. At the same time, the tin soldier melted into the coals, bound forever together with his beautiful ballerina.

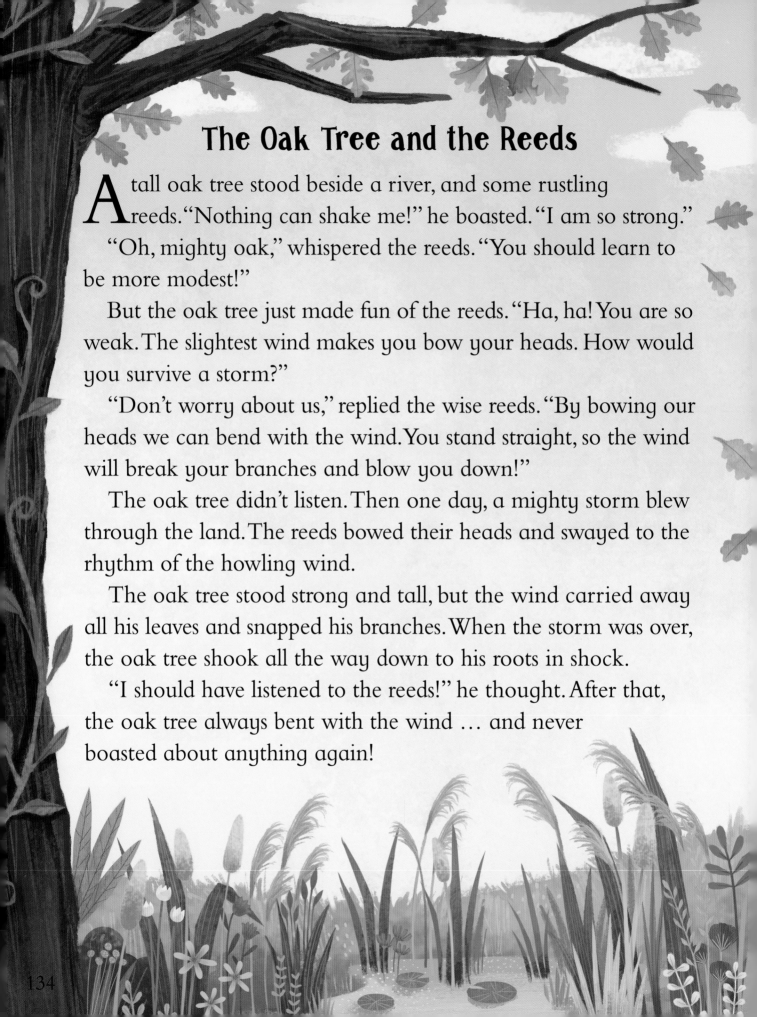

The Oak Tree and the Reeds

A tall oak tree stood beside a river, and some rustling reeds. "Nothing can shake me!" he boasted. "I am so strong."

"Oh, mighty oak," whispered the reeds. "You should learn to be more modest!"

But the oak tree just made fun of the reeds. "Ha, ha! You are so weak. The slightest wind makes you bow your heads. How would you survive a storm?"

"Don't worry about us," replied the wise reeds. "By bowing our heads we can bend with the wind. You stand straight, so the wind will break your branches and blow you down!"

The oak tree didn't listen. Then one day, a mighty storm blew through the land. The reeds bowed their heads and swayed to the rhythm of the howling wind.

The oak tree stood strong and tall, but the wind carried away all his leaves and snapped his branches. When the storm was over, the oak tree shook all the way down to his roots in shock.

"I should have listened to the reeds!" he thought. After that, the oak tree always bent with the wind … and never boasted about anything again!

The Old Man and his Gold

Once upon a time, an old man who hated spending his gold dug a hole in his garden to bury it. Every day, he would go outside, dig up his gold, count it all, then bury it again. "I'm so rich!" he thought boastfully.

One day, a thief saw what the old man was doing. He waited until nightfall, then returned to the garden and stole the old man's gold.

When the old man discovered the empty hole, he cried out in alarm. The neighbors ran into the garden to find out what had happened. The old man explained it to them.

"Did you never spend any of your gold?" asked one neighbor.

The old man shook his head. "Not a penny!" he replied.

"Well," the neighbor continued, "you might as well just pretend it's still there. Your gold was no use to you anyway!"

The Open Road

One bright summer morning, Mole said, "Ratty, I want to ask you a favor."

"Why, certainly," said Ratty, who was sitting by the river.

"Well, what I wanted to ask you is, can we call on Mr. Toad? I've heard so much about him."

"Get the boat out and we'll paddle up there at once. Toad is always in and will be delighted to meet you."

Rat and Mole rounded a bend in the river and came in sight of a handsome old stone house.

"There's Toad Hall," said Ratty. "It is the biggest house in these parts." They moored the boat on the bank and started to walk toward Toad Hall.

"Hooray!" cried Toad as the three animals shook paws.

"The very fellows I wanted to see! You have to help me sort out something really important!"

"It's about boating, I suppose?" asked the Rat.

"Forget about that!" cried the Toad. "I gave that up ages ago. Now I've discovered the real thing. Come with me!"

He led the way to the stable yard, where, in the open, was a shiny new gypsy caravan with red wheels.

"There!" cried Toad. "There's the real life. A home away from home, traveling the road without a care in the world."

Mole followed Toad up the steps and inside. Ratty remained where he was, hands thrust deep in his pockets.

"I've thought of everything," cried Toad. He pulled open a cupboard. "Here's everything we could possibly want to eat." Then he threw open a closet. "Here's all the clothes we need! We must start at once."

"I beg your pardon," said Rat, "but did I hear you say 'we'?"

"Now, dear Ratty," said Toad calmly, "don't get on your high horse. You have to come."

"I'm not coming, and that is that," said the Rat.

"Me neither," said Mole, siding loyally with Ratty.

"All the same … " he added, "it does sound like fun."

"I'll say it would be fun," said Toad, and he began to paint the joys of caravanning. In no time at all, even Rat was interested.

And so it was that all three friends set off that afternoon to discover the joys of caravanning on the open road.

"This is the life, eh!" said a sleepy Toad that evening, when they stopped for supper. "Better than talking about your river, eh, Ratty?"

"I don't talk about my river, Toad," replied Rat. "You know I don't. But I think about it," he added quietly, "all the time."

Mole reached out and squeezed Ratty's paw. "Dear Ratty," he whispered. "Should we run away tomorrow and go back to our dear old hole on the river?"

"No, we'll see it out," whispered the Rat. "We must stick by Toad until he's over this craze. It won't take long."

The end was nearer than even Rat suspected. Next morning, Mole turned the horse's head toward their first really wide main road. In the distance they heard a faint warning hum, like the buzz of a bee. An instant later, with a loud BEEP!, a whirl of wind, and a blast of sound, an automobile tore past.

The old horse who was pulling the caravan let out a whinny of fear, reared, then plunged and bucked, driving the caravan into a ditch, where it landed with a huge crash.

Ratty danced with rage. "You villains!" he shouted, shaking both fists. "You scoundrels, you … you … road hogs!"

Mole looked down at the caravan. Panels and windows were smashed, the axles hopelessly bent, and cans of food were scattered about. And Toad? Toad sat in the middle of the road staring in the direction of the now disappeared car.

Rat shook him by the shoulder. "Come on, Toad, do get up!"

But Toad wouldn't move. "Glorious!" he murmured. "That's the way to travel. Oh, bliss! Oh, beep beep!"

"Oh, drat Toad!" said Ratty crossly. "I'm done with him! I've seen it all before. He's off on to a new craze. He'll be in a dream for days. We'll just have to get him to his feet, then make our way to the nearest town and catch a train home."

"Now, look here, Toad!" said Ratty. "You'll have to make a complaint against that scoundrel and his car."

"Me? Complain?" murmured Toad. "I wouldn't dream of it. I'm going to order one right away!"

Ratty sighed. Some things would never change.

Island Adventure

Captain Nat and his friends were sailing in their boat, looking for adventures. Nat scanned the sea with his telescope. "Land ho!" he shouted. "There's an island straight ahead!"

They dropped the anchor and rowed to shore in a little dinghy. Airplanes roared overhead and a steam train chugged across the island. There were shiny sportscars racing around a track, and speedboats pulling water-skiers through the waves.

"What an amazing island!" said First Mate Peggy. "Time to explore. Let's go!"

The crew jumped into the little blue train and the whistle blew. Chugga-chugga, chugga-chugga. They were off on a tour of the island. It was filled with exciting vehicles of every shape and size.

There were helicopters, tractors, and motorcycles, and there was even a submarine sitting in the harbor! But best of all, they were all just the right size for children, and a big sign said "No Grown-ups Allowed".

"Let's have a competition," said Chief Cook Corin. "The first one to have a ride in all the vehicles is the winner!"

Captain Nat and his cabin boys Jake and Fraser jumped into an airplane. First Mate Peggy leaped onto a motorcycle and Chief Cook Corin took the train. Vroom vroom! Zoom zoom! Soon the crew was whizzing all over the island, trying the fastest, loudest vehicles they could find. It was a close race! They all arrived back on the beach at the same time, and raced over the sand to the dinghy. But the winner was Captain Nat.

"Three cheers for the captain!" shouted First Mate Peggy. "But what's his prize?"

"I'm allowed to steer the ship home," said Captain Nat with a grin. "Anchors aweigh!"

I Love My Grandma

Little Hedgehog and Grandma Hedgehog loved to play hide-and-go-seek together. One day, when Grandma went to find Little Hedgehog to help her make a picnic, he hid behind a bush.

"Where can Little Hedgehog be?" said Grandma.

Little Hedgehog giggled.

"Oh, well. I shall just have to make the picnic myself," said Grandma.

Little Hedgehog followed closely behind Grandma.

"I wish Little Hedgehog were here to help me pick juicy blackberries," said Grandma.

When she wasn't looking, Little Hedgehog picked the biggest blackberries he could reach and put them into Grandma's basket!

"What a lot of berries!" said Grandma, surprised. "I have enough for baking now."

Little Hedgehog scampered into Grandma's kitchen to find the best place to hide. He crouched down low, so that Grandma couldn't see him.

"If only Little Hedgehog were here to help me," said Grandma.

Little Hedgehog licked his lips as Grandma Hedgehog poured sweet, scrumptious honey into her mixing bowl.

When Grandma wasn't looking, Little Hedgehog crept out from his hiding place to taste the honey. Then he quickly hid again.

"Someone has been tasting my honey," said Grandma. "And they have left sticky footprints!"

Grandma followed the teeny-tiny, sticky footprints across the kitchen and out into the garden.

"Someone has been playing hide-and-go-seek with me!" she said, smiling.

The sticky footprints went around and around the garden, and stopped by the flowerpots.

"I've found you, Little Hedgehog!" cried Grandma.

But Little Hedgehog wasn't behind the flowerpots! He was ... inside one!

"Surprise!" laughed Little Hedgehog.

"Well done, Little Hedgehog," said Grandma. "You're the best at hide-and-go-seek. I hope you're hungry, because our picnic is ready!"

"I am hungry," said Little Hedgehog, eagerly looking around the garden. "But where is the picnic?"

Grandma giggled. "You have to find it!" she said.

Little Hedgehog searched around the garden, and soon found honey cookies and fruit salad.

Then, Grandma brought out a giant blackberry cake.

"Yum! I love Grandma's picnics!" Little Hedgehog shouted happily. "And ... I love my grandma!"

The Smallest Knight

Freddie lived in the royal castle, just like all the Queen's knights. Every day, he joined in with the parades and watched all the jousting games. Every night, he dreamed of being one of the Queen's knights.

"I know I could be a good knight," he said. But Freddie wasn't a knight. He was a servant boy. And nobody had ever heard of a servant boy being made a knight.

One day, Freddie was trying on a knight's helmet when the Queen came in, followed by all her knights.

"The key to the kingdom has been lost," she said. "Without it, nothing will work properly. It must be found!"

"I will find the key," said Freddie, nervously piping up.

The other knights didn't know who he was. "You're much too small to be a real knight," they said, laughing.

But the Queen nodded at Freddie. "If you find it, I will make you one of my knights," she said.

The knights crawled through fields and climbed trees. They dived into lakes and peered under bushes. But none of them found the key.

At the end of the day, weary and glum, they rode back to the castle. "Your key has vanished forever," they told the Queen.

"Nonsense!" cried a voice. The smallest knight strode forward and held up a shining key. "It had slipped through a crack in the castle floorboards," he said. "Sometimes it helps to be small!"

"Please take off your helmet," said the Queen. When the knight obeyed, everyone gasped. It was Freddie!

Smiling, the Queen lifted her golden sword and touched Freddie on each shoulder.

"Arise, Sir Freddie," she said.

Everyone cheered. From now on, they knew that even a small servant could be a heroic knight!

The Balloon Ride

Zach's big sister Laurel looked sad, so Zach gave her a big hug. "What's the matter?" he asked.

"All the other children at school have been to see their dads at work," Laurel said. "I've never seen our dad at work."

Their dad didn't go to work in an office. He didn't do any of the things that other dads did. You see, their dad was a pilot.

"I know he flies airplanes," said Laurel. "But I don't even know what his airplane looks like. I wish we could visit him at work."

"Maybe we can!" Zach exclaimed. He threw open his toy box and rummaged inside. Then he pulled out his toy hot-air balloon. "What if we could make this balloon fly?" he said.

Laurel's eyes sparkled with excitement, and they both sat in the basket. "We fit inside, but we're going to need a bigger balloon," Zach said.

"I know where Mom keeps some old curtains," said Laurel. "I'll go and get them!"

Zach and Laurel made a new balloon and tied it to the basket. Then Zach used Mom's blow-dryer to fill the balloon with hot air. It grew bigger...and bigger...and bigger...until at last it lifted upward. Zach and Laurel were carried into the sky.

WHOOSH! Airplanes zoomed all around them. Laurel squealed with excitement. Then a huge passenger jet whizzed along beside them. The pilot was waving and smiling.

"Look, Laurel!" cried Zach. "It's Dad!"

The children waved, and their dad waved back. So did all the astonished passengers who were going on vacation! Then the airplane flew on, and Laurel threw her arms around Zach.

"Thank you for thinking of this!" she exclaimed. "You're the best little brother in the world!"

How the Tiger Got His Stripes

A very long time ago, when the tiger had no stripes upon his back and the rabbit still had a long tail, there was a tiger who owned a farm. Since his farm was very overgrown with underbrush, the tiger decided to look for a worker to clear the ground for him so he could plant his crops.

The tiger called all the animals together. "I need a good workman to clear the underbrush. I will give an ox in payment to whoever does the work."

A monkey, a goat, and an armadillo applied for the job, but when the tiger tried them out, they didn't do the work to his satisfaction, and he dismissed them all without payment.

Finally a little rabbit applied for the position. The tiger laughed at him, "You are too small to do the work!"

But since there were no other applicants for the job, the tiger decided to give the rabbit the job.

The rabbit worked hard and soon he had cleared a large portion of the ground. For the next few days the rabbit continued to work hard until he had cleared all the ground. The tiger was very pleased. He gave the rabbit the ox as promised.

The rabbit took the ox and went off to find a spot to kill it and have his lunch. Just as he was about to eat the ox, the tiger appeared from the bushes nearby.

"O, rabbit, I'm so very hungry!" cried the tiger. "Look, you can see my ribs. Since you are such a good friend of mine, won't you be so kind as to give me a piece of your ox to eat?"

The rabbit gave the tiger a piece of the ox. The tiger devoured it immediately.

"Is that all you are going to give me to eat?" asked the sly tiger.

The tiger looked so big and savage that the rabbit didn't dare to refuse him any more of the ox. Soon the tiger had devoured the entire ox, leaving only a tiny morsel for the poor rabbit.

The rabbit was furious with the tiger. A few days later, he went to a place near the tiger's farm and began cutting down big staves of wood.

The tiger saw the rabbit and wondered what he was doing.

"Oh, haven't you heard?" said the rabbit. "The order has gone forth that every beast should build a stockade around themselves, to protect them from hunters."

The tiger was alarmed. "Oh, no! Rabbit, what shall I do?" he cried. "I don't know how to build a stockade. Since you are my dear friend, won't you help me first before you build your own stockade?"

The rabbit sighed and agreed to help him. He built a strong stockade around the tiger using sharp sticks, and fastened more sticks over the top until the tiger was completely shut in. Then he left.

The tiger waited and waited for something to happen. Nothing did and he grew very hungry and thirsty.

Then he heard some animals passing by. It was the monkey, goat, and armadillo.

"Oh, dear friends," roared the tiger. "Has the danger passed? Can you help me out of here?"

The animals were still angry at the tiger about the work on his farm. "Yes, the danger has passed," they lied. "Let the one who got you in there help you out." And they walked away.

The desperate tiger threw himself again and again, with all his might, at the bars of his stockade, until finally, he broke through. The sticks were so sharp, that the unfortunate tiger was badly cut on both sides of his body.

And that is how the tiger got his stripes.

Monsters Always ...

All mommies want their children to have good manners. But good monster manners are the opposite of good human manners.

"Mess up your toys," Mommy Monster said to Baby Monster each day. "Spill more food on the floor. Your hands are too clean!"

But Baby Monster just wanted to be neat and tidy.

"I'll take him to the park," said Daddy Monster. "Baby Monster will soon see how much fun it is to get messy!"

Daddy Monster took Baby Monster to the muddiest, slimiest pond in the park. "Let's collect waterweeds!" he said. SQUELCH! They waded in and threw mud at each other.

"What a good little monster!" said the passersby.

Next, Daddy Monster put a picnic rug on the soggiest grass he could find. He opened the picnic hamper. "Tuck in, Baby Monster!" he said.

What a messy picnic! Squashy, ripe peaches dribbled down their chins. Cream puffs exploded over their faces. Sticky honey sandwiches stuck to their fur. Daddy Monster blew bubbles in the chocolate milkshake and drenched them both.

Giggling, Baby Monster jumped on Daddy Monster and gave him a big tickle. They rolled around in the soggy grass and fell into a bog with a big, squelchy PLOP! Daddy Monster felt very happy that Baby Monster had finally learned some good monster manners. But then …

"I want to go home now," said Baby Monster.

"So you can roll around and make the carpet muddy?" asked Daddy Monster.

"No," said Baby Monster, laughing. "So I can take a bath and get clean again!"

Oh no!

The Hero of Bramble Farm

Everyone at Bramble Farm was asleep. Everyone, that is, except a little lamb called George. A noise from outside the barn had woken him.

"What was that?" he whispered.

THUMP! BANG! George got up and tiptoed out of the barn. Two men were grabbing the farmer's tools and stuffing them into sacks.

"Burglars!" George exclaimed.

How could one little lamb stop two big burglars? Then he had an idea. Maybe he could make the burglars think that other animals were there too.

George took a deep breath. "BAA! NEIGH! OINK! MOOOO!" He made the noise of every farm animal he knew.

"Run!" shouted the burglars. "They're after us!"

George's clever noisy idea had saved the day!

Moo!

Neigh!

Oink!

Team Tractor

There were lots of big, shiny tractors in the store. Farmers came in every day to buy them. But one tractor never seemed to get noticed.

"I wish I could work on a farm," said the little green tractor. "My cab is shiny and new. But no one looks at me."

One day, a farmer came in with his son Jamie. The farmer's tractor had broken, and he needed a new one to plant a field with seeds.

"Please!" thought the little green tractor. "Please buy me!"

The farmer was looking at the big machines, but Jamie stared at the little tractor. "You're just the right size for our little farm," he grinned, and called his dad over to see it.

"What a perfect tractor," the farmer agreed.

So they took the little green tractor home, and together they planted the field of seeds in record time!

The Donkey and the Pet Dog

A long time ago, a man lived in a small cottage with his pet dog. He kept a donkey in a stable in the backyard. The donkey had to help the man work the land and carry heavy loads. The donkey didn't mind working so hard, because he always had a warm bed to sleep in and plenty of oats and hay to eat.

Every day, the donkey couldn't help but notice that the dog didn't have any work to do. Instead, the dog played all day and his master gave him treats to eat and lots of cuddles. The donkey was very jealous of the dog's easy life.

One day, the donkey had had enough. "It's not fair!" he shouted. "I work hard every day, while that dog gets all the attention for doing nothing!"

The donkey galloped into the cottage. He kicked up his hooves and brayed loudly. Then he tried to jump onto the man's lap, as he had seen the dog do many times before. But, of course, he was too big. The donkey broke the chair and all the dishes on the table.

"Look what you've done!" shouted the man.

The donkey bowed his head in shame.
"I just wanted to be treated in the same way
as your dog," he said.

The man didn't want his donkey to be unhappy.
So, from then on, the man, the donkey and the dog all
helped with the work … and they even had time to play and
rest a bit afterward, too.

Walk the Plank

One morning, Erik the pirate captain got out of the wrong side of his hammock.

"I'm fed up with searching for treasure and never finding it," he said. "Being a pirate is no fun any more!"

Erik thought that a few games might bring the fun back. He ordered his crew to start playing. They tried Tiddlywinks, Checkers, and Fish, but it was no use.

"You're all cheating!" Erik roared. "You no-good pirates. I don't want games! I want treasure and ships to sink!"

"Pieces of eight!" squawked his parrot.

"Yo ho ho!" shouted the pirates.

Then Erik had a great idea. "I know what will cheer me up," he said to himself. "I'll make every single silly pirate walk the plank!"

SPLASH! One by one, the pirates stomped down the plank and jumped into the sea. SPLASH! Erik felt better already.

158

"We'll teach him a lesson!" the pirates spluttered, gathering together in the water.

The pirates climbed up a rope that hung over the side of the ship. Erik was standing beside the plank and singing.

"Ha ha ha!" he chortled. "They all made a silly splash! Ho ho ho!"

The pirates tiptoed up behind him. On the first mate's signal, they all shouted "BOO!"

Erik let out a yell of surprise and tumbled off the plank. SPLASH!

Giggling, the other pirates jumped off the plank too, dive bombing into the water with their captain. Erik spluttered and laughed as they splashed each other. All his grumpy feelings had disappeared. "Yo ho ho!" he shouted. "The life of a pirate is the best fun ever!"

The Magic Merry-Go-Round

Danny didn't enjoy going shopping with Mom. It took much too long! She always wanted to go into every single store in town. They had already been into the grocery store, the clothes store, and the shoe store. The only store they hadn't gone into was the toy store. They had met nine of Mom's friends, and she had spent much too long talking to them.

"I just want to have another look at those skirts," said Mom. Danny was about to groan when he saw something exciting. There was a large brand-new merry-go-round—right in the middle of Main Street!

"Mom!" he whispered, tugging at her coat. "Mom! Can I go on that?" Mom agreed, and Danny raced over to the merry-go-round. It had blue and yellow stripes, with white, prancing horses. Danny bought a ticket and climbed onto one of the horses. It had a yellow saddle and one leg held up in the air.

"You look like a fast horse," said Danny, patting its mane. The music began and the horses started to move.

"Giddy up!" shouted Danny. "Faster!" The merry-go-round whirled so fast that soon the town and the shops were a blur.

When the ride slowed down, the town had completely disappeared! Instead, Danny found himself in the middle of a magical fairground wonderland. There were amazing rides all around. He could hardly wait to try them out. As he ran through the fairground he saw faces that he knew. The wolf from Red Riding Hood was testing his strength. Little Bo Peep was taking a break from searching for her sheep, and Georgie Porgie was munching on some pie.

Danny whizzed down the big slide. He rode on dancing bees and whirled around on the dish that ran away with the spoon. There was a pirate's treasure rollercoaster and a boat ride around the fairground. He flew down the monkey slides and flew up and around on the Itsy Bitsy spider ride. It was the best fun Danny had ever had!

After Danny had been on every ride twice, he followed one of the three little pigs to a market. There were stands selling jars of delicious honey, gingerbread men, and iced cupcakes, as well as elegant hats and the biggest, brightest balloons that Danny had ever seen. He bought armfuls of crusty bread, candy, pies and cookies, and a basket of ripe, delicious fruit and vegetables. When he couldn't carry any more, he knew that it was time to go home.

Danny climbed back onto the prancing white horse, holding on tightly to his packages. The horses started to move. Faster! Faster! The merry-go-round turned the fairground into a blur, and then slowed down. Danny was back on Main Street again. He slipped off the horse and waved at Mom, who was coming out of the store.

"Goodness me, where did you get all that food?" she exclaimed. "I've only been in the store for two minutes!"

Danny looked back at the merry-go-round and grinned. "I'll tell you all about it, Mom," he said. "As long as you promise to bring me back here tomorrow!"

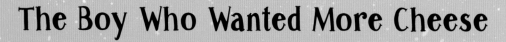

The Boy Who Wanted More Cheese

Klaas Van Bommel was a 12-year-old Dutch boy who lived with his family on a farm. There was always plenty to eat—wonderful breads, potatoes, and Klaas' favorite, cheese. Klaas loved cheese more than any other food. At mealtimes he would always try to get his sisters to give him their portions, until his mother scolded him.

"Klaas, you are going to burst if you eat any more cheese," she cried.

Even when his stomach was full, Klass still wanted more cheese. He was a good boy in all other ways, but his love of cheese always led him into trouble.

One night when he had been sent to bed early for taking his sisters' cheese again, Klaas lay sulking on his bed, looking out of his window.

Suddenly, he saw little lights moving around a tree in the yard, and he heard a tiny, tinkling voice.

"There's plenty of cheese. Come with us."

164

Klaas had heard people talk about the fairies in the woods. He quietly crept out of the house and followed the whispering voice. Under the tree he was surrounded by dozens of tiny fairies. "Come dance with us," they sang out. "There is plenty of cheese here!"

Klaas danced all night until the sun began to rise. Then he fell into a dreamy sleep, in which he was surrounded by hundreds of different cheeses. The cheese tasted delicious. Klaas ate until he was full, but the cheese kept coming and started tumbling down on top of him! As he screamed in terror, he woke up. Klass was lying on the grass under a tree. He looked around him. There were no fairies or cheese.

Klaas never told anyone about his strange cheesey night, and from then on he only ate cheese in small amounts!

The Wolf in Sheep's Clothing

Night after night, a hungry wolf prowled around a flock of sheep, looking for one he could eat, but the shepherd always spotted him and chased him away.

One night, when the wolf was on the point of giving up, he found an old sheepskin that the shepherd had thrown aside. Grinning, the wolf pulled the skin carefully over himself so that none of his fur showed under the woolly fleece. Then he slowly strolled into the middle of the flock.

After a while, a lamb came up to the wolf. Thinking the wolf was its mother the lamb followed the wolf into the woods. Poor little lamb! The hungry wolf gobbled it up!

On the following night, and for several nights after that, the cunning wolf used his clever disguise, feasting on the sheep whenever he pleased.

And the moral of the story is: things are not always as they appear to be.

The Man, the Bird, and the Ogres

One day a man went into the forest to cut timber. He worked hard all day and was about to set off home when he saw a sickly bird, quivering on the path in front of him. He stopped to give it some food and water.

"You have been so kind," chirped the bird. "One day I will help you too."

The man smiled, but he didn't really believe that such a tiny creature could help him.

Several weeks later, when the man was in the forest again, four huge ogres came running toward him through the trees. He was terrified. He scrambled up a tree to hide. Suddenly, a little bird appeared. It started singing sweetly, while flying from tree to tree. The singing distracted the ogres and they started following the delightful sound.

The man quietly slipped down the tree and ran all the way home. The little bird he once helped had now saved him from the ogres.

167

The Frog Kingdom

Felipe the frog was sitting beside the river with his friends when he saw a purple lily pad.

"First frog on the pad rules!" he shouted as he leaped. But as soon as his feet touched the lily pad, it shot off down the river. Felipe held on tight as the lily pad pushed through the leaves of a willow tree hanging over the water. On the other side, the lily pad suddenly slowed and things seemed different. Frogs that Felipe didn't know were cheering and waving to him from the bank. The lily pad stopped and Felipe sprang off.

"Welcome to your kingdom," said a tall frog, putting a crown on Felipe's head. "Three cheers for the king!"

Felipe looked around in amazement as the crowd led him through the watery streets of a green city, filled with froggy houses. Everyone came out to wave. Felipe's palace was at the center, filled with velvety lily pads and cool, bubbling ponds.

"Your wish is our command!" said a frog in red uniform.

"Then I wish for a grand party," said Felipe. "Everyone in the kingdom is invited!"

The streets were filled with ribbons and balloons. Candies were scattered from rooftops and cherry cola flowed from the fountains. Music filled the air and King Felipe danced with everyone. He was dancing beside the river when his foot slipped and he fell onto the purple lily pad. At once, it began to float back up the river.

"I don't want to go!" Felipe cried as the lily pad pushed back through the willow leaves.

His friends were waiting on the riverbank.

"I'm a king!" Felipe cried. "I rule the Frog Kingdom!"

His friends laughed, but Felipe knew that he hadn't been dreaming. He was still wearing his crown!

The Bravest Best Friend

Mitch Mouse and Micky Mole were best friends. They played together every day. But one day, Mitch and Micky had an argument.

"Mice aren't as brave as moles," said Micky, puffing out his velvety chest.

"Moles are much more nervous than mice," Mitch replied.

"Scaredy cat!" said Micky Mole. "You're frightened of loud noises!"

"I'm not a scaredy cat!" Mitch Mouse squeaked. "You're the scaredy cat! You're scared of the sunshine!"

"Oh no I'm not," huffed Micky. "I have an idea. Let's have a bravery competition. Whoever can do the most brave things today is the winner, and the bravest best friend of all time."

Mitch agreed, and set off to prove how brave he was.

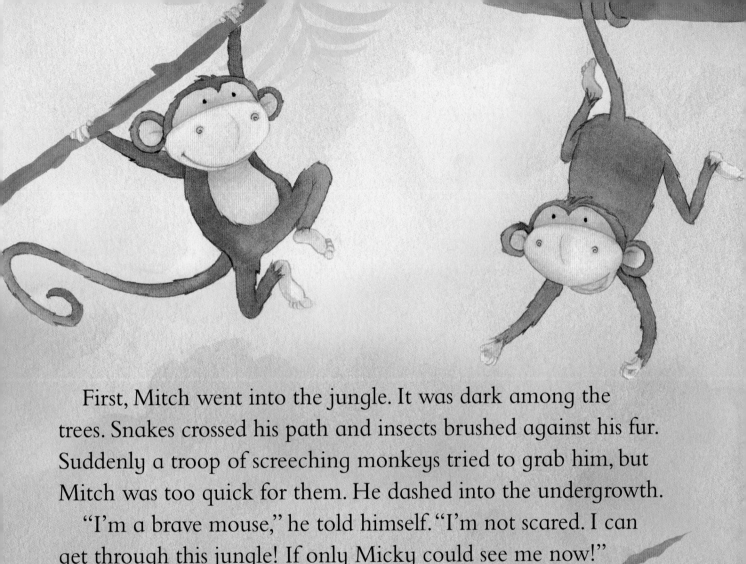

First, Mitch went into the jungle. It was dark among the trees. Snakes crossed his path and insects brushed against his fur. Suddenly a troop of screeching monkeys tried to grab him, but Mitch was too quick for them. He dashed into the undergrowth.

"I'm a brave mouse," he told himself. "I'm not scared. I can get through this jungle! If only Micky could see me now!"

At last, Mitch reached a little town on the other side of the jungle. He was tired and hungry, but he kept walking. Then he saw a couple of pampered cats sipping milk and nibbling cubes of cheese.

"Cats eating cheese? Whatever next!" he exclaimed to himself.

His tummy rumbled when he looked at the delicious morsels of cheese. They smelled so good! There was only one thing for it. He had to have the cheese.

Mitch took a deep breath. "I'm a brave mouse!" he muttered. Then he ran out in front of the cats, made faces at them, and did a silly dance. They gawped at him in amazement. They had never seen a mouse do that before! While they were staring, Mitch darted forward, filled his arms with cheese, and ran.

It took the cats a few seconds to believe their eyes. Had a mouse really just stolen their food? They looked at each other, yowled loudly, popped out their claws, and chased after Mitch.

What a chase it was! Mitch raced through every alley in the town. He dived under garbage can lids and darted into drains. But the cats always sniffed him out. Mitch's legs were aching and he knew that he couldn't run much farther. Then he saw an owl swooping down to catch him. He was scared he was going to be eaten. But faster than lightning, he sprang onto the owl's back and hitched a lift all the way to Micky's house. He couldn't wait to tell his best friend all about his day and he was sure all his adventures would make him the winner of the bravery competition! As he opened the door he could hear loud snoring. Micky was fast asleep, exhausted from his own brave adventures!

The Wolf and the Seven Young Kids

An old mother goat lived with her seven little kids. One day she went out and left them alone, warning them that the wolf might come, and that they must not let him in.

"Don't let that rascal trick you," she said. "He has a gruff old voice and his paws are as black as coal. That is how you will recognize him."

Sure enough, not long after the mother goat had left, there was a knock, knock, knock! at the door.

"Let me in," said a gruff old voice.

"We know it's you, wolf," said the kids. "You have such a gruff old voice."

So the wolf went away and ate some chalk to soften his voice. Then he went back to the goats' house and knocked on the door.

"Let me in," he said with his smooth, chalky voice. But the seven young kids noticed his black paws poking through a crack in the bottom of the door. "We know it's you, wolf," said the kids. "Your paws are as black as coal."

So the wolf went away and covered his paws with white flour. Then he went back to the goats' house and knocked on the door.

"Let me in," he said. His voice was not gruff and his paws were

not black, so the seven young kids opened the door and let him in.

In one huge gulp, the wolf ate six of the young kids, but the seventh one hid in a cupboard.

When the mother goat returned home, the seventh kid ran out from the cupboard and told her all about the wolf.

"Oh, my poor babies!" cried the mother goat. "We must go and find that wicked wolf." And they set off to look for him.

They found the old rascal sleeping beneath a tree. The mother goat carefully cut open the wolf's big fat stomach with a snip, snip! and six young kids hopped out alive and well!

Then she picked up six stones and put them in the wolf's stomach before sewing it back up again.

The wolf woke up feeling thirsty and went to get some water from the well. But the weight of the stones made him fall down the well, and he landed in the water with a splash! And the wolf with the gruff old voice and paws as black as coal was never seen again.

One Good Turn

Once, there was a king who was famous for his wisdom. He seemed to know everything and everyone's secrets. But the king had a secret of his own. In his palace, there was a room that no one else was allowed to enter.

One evening, while cleaning the king's boots, a servant was overcome with curiosity about the forbidden room. He peeked inside and saw a white snake, trapped in a big, glass tank.

"Please help me," hissed the snake. "The king has kept me here for years. I have to tell him everything he wants to know. But I just want to be free."

The servant was startled to hear the snake talk, but he did as he was asked.

The white snake slithered out, and said, "Thank you for freeing me. I will grant you a magical power in return."

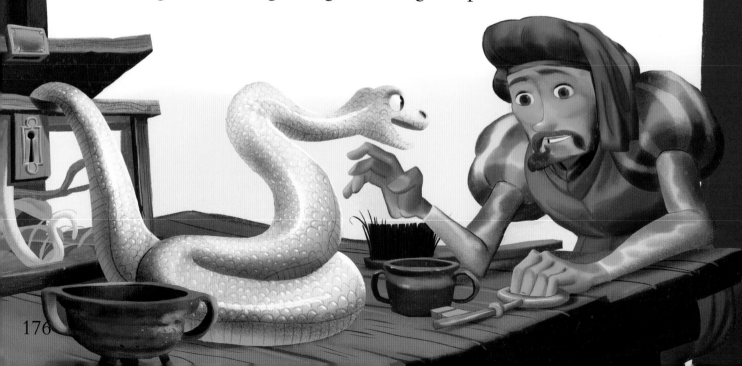

Suddenly, the servant could hear lots of strange whispery voices. The snake had given him a magical power to understand animals. Now the servant knew how the king had become so wise … the white snake was magical!

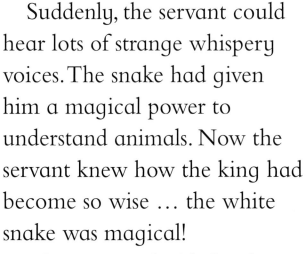

The servant decided to leave the palace before the king could find out what he had done. As he sat by a river to rest, he noticed three fish tangled in a net.

"Please help us!" they cried.

The servant heard their plea and freed them straightaway.

Then he continued on his journey. On the path ahead, the servant saw three baby ravens that had fallen from their nest.

"Who will help us get food now?" they chirped.

The servant heard their cries and gave them some of his food.

After several days, the servant came to a kingdom where the king had promised his daughter's hand in marriage to anyone who could complete a difficult task.

The servant decided to try his luck.

The king threw a ring into the sea and told him to retrieve it. The servant began to swim out into the choppy waves. Suddenly, he saw three fish. They had the ring and gave it to him.

"One good deed deserves another," said the fish.

The king told the servant he could marry the princess, but when the princess saw the servant, she didn't want to marry him.

"If you bring me the golden apple from the tree of life, I will marry you," she said, thinking that the servant would never be able to do this.

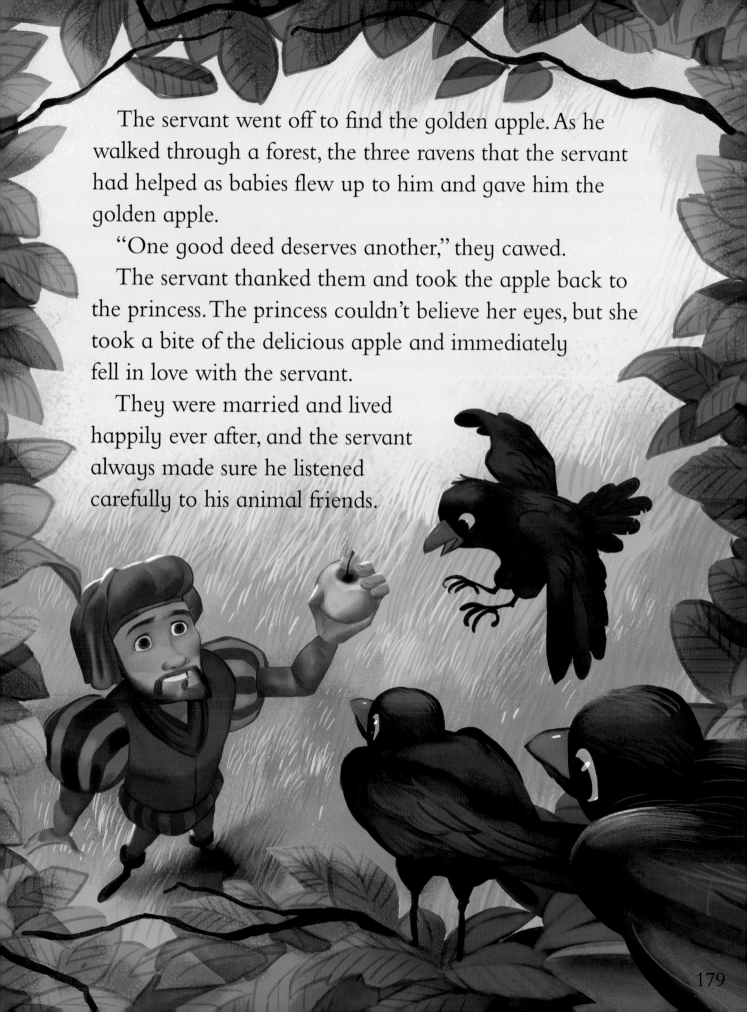

The servant went off to find the golden apple. As he walked through a forest, the three ravens that the servant had helped as babies flew up to him and gave him the golden apple.

"One good deed deserves another," they cawed.

The servant thanked them and took the apple back to the princess. The princess couldn't believe her eyes, but she took a bite of the delicious apple and immediately fell in love with the servant.

They were married and lived happily ever after, and the servant always made sure he listened carefully to his animal friends.

179

Bath Time for Bertie

Mommy Elephant swayed her trunk as she walked through the long grass toward the trees lining the river.

"Bertie!" she called loudly. "It's bathtime. We need to go to the river before the light fades."

Bertie the baby elephant flapped his ears in a panic, and ran to hide behind the large baobab tree.

"I'm not here!" called Bertie.

"I can see your little swishy tail!" laughed Mommy.

Bertie loved living on the vast African plain. He loved running through the long grass. And best of all he loved rolling in the dusty mud with Mommy.

But he did not like bath time at all!

"I'm afraid of the river," sobbed Bertie. "The water moves so quickly. I'm frightened it will sweep me away!"

"Don't worry, I'll stay by your side the whole time, I promise," Mommy said, gently.

Holding on to Mommy's tail, Bertie slowly waded into the shallow water by the river bank.

"If you put your feet like this," explained Mommy Elephant, showing Bertie how to stand in the water, "you won't fall over."

Bertie moved his feet. The water swirled past, but he didn't fall.

Mommy gently sprayed some water over Bertie's head.

Bertie giggled loudly. The cool water felt lovely as it trickled down his back.

"Maybe bath time isn't so bad after all!" laughed Bertie. "I can't wait for my bath tomorrow!"

The Fir Tree

In the very heart of a beautiful forest, there stood a little fir tree. Although it was still young, the fir tree grew straight and true. Its trunk was strong and its branches were mossy green and studded with hundreds of tiny fir cones. It had enough sunshine to warm its cones but also shelter from the wind and rain. Fine trees towered all around it, standing side by side like brothers.

The little fir tree could watch the sun rise in the sky every day and it was surrounded by pretty flowers. These things should have made the fir tree feel contented, but it was impatient and dissatisfied. It didn't like being the smallest tree in the forest.

Every day the fir tree found something to moan about—the children running happily through the forest, the songbirds, the changing seasons. Nothing made the little fir tree happy and it spent its time wishing the days and months away.

"Hurry up, branches. Grow, grow, grow!" it complained. "Why does it take so long?"

"You are still young," murmured the wind as it whistled through the fir tree's branches. "These days are precious. You should make the most of them."

But the fir tree didn't want to listen. Year by year, it kept growing, and still nothing pleased it. It watched its neighboring trees being felled by the woodcutters who came every year.

"Why don't they choose me?" it complained. "I'm every bit as handsome. Where are they taking them?"

"It's Christmas time. Those trees are off to town," chirped the sparrows. "Soon they'll be placed in a room and covered in beautiful decorations."

The little fir tree thought this sounded like the greatest honor any tree could wish for! From that moment on, the fir tree yearned to be a Christmas tree.

And then, the little fir tree's turn came! The woodcutters chopped it down and threw it onto a truck. The fir tree could hardly breathe from the weight of the other trees on it, and it was still feeling faint from the pain of the ax cutting it down. Suddenly it felt sad to be leaving its forest home.

Later that day, the fir tree found itself in a grand room, standing in a pot and covered in glittering decorations, presents, candies, and lights. It felt marvelous!

"I wonder how long I shall be on display like this?" it pondered happily. "All winter perhaps? Maybe all summer, too?"

But the very next day the children came and grabbed the presents and candies from its branches, and a man came and took down the lights and decorations, before throwing the little fir tree out into a yard.

The following morning the fir tree was cut into logs for the fire.

"If only I had enjoyed my time on the hillside instead of wasting it," it sighed. "Every moment should have been a treasure."

As the fir tree melted into the fire, it saw things clearly for the first time and it gave thanks for the beauty it had seen in its life.

The Fox and the Tiger

One day a fox was walking through the forest when he met a tiger. The fox was afraid, but he said, "My dear sir, you must not think that you are the only king of the beasts!"

The tiger bared his teeth, but the fox bravely continued.

"Your courage does not compare with mine. Walk behind me and I will show you. If any animal does not fear me, then you may devour me!"

The tiger decided to play along with the fox. As they walked through the forest, every animal that saw them ran away.

"You see!" the fox cried triumphantly. "All those animals saw me and ran away before they even caught sight of you!"

The tiger took one look at the fox and ran away himself! He had seen how terrified the other animals were, but he did not realize that it was him, and not the fox, they were really afraid of!

The Lion's Bad Breath

Lion was in a bad mood. Just that morning his wife had told him his breath smelled. He pretended he didn't care, but secretly he was worried, so he summoned three of his advisors—Sheep, Wolf, and Fox.

"Tell me, Sheep," growled Lion, "does my breath smell?"

The Sheep thought Lion wanted to know the truth, so she said, "Your Majesty, your breath smells terrible."

Lion was so angry he sent the poor sheep away forever! Then he asked Wolf, "Do you think my breath smells?"

"Your Majesty!" the trembling Wolf cried, "Your breath smells as sweet as the flowers in spring, as fresh … "

"Liar!" roared Lion before Wolf could finish, and sent him off too.

"So, Fox, does my breath smell?" said Lion menacingly.

Thinking quickly, the frightened Fox coughed and sneezed and blew her nose. In a hoarse voice, she croaked, "I am so sorry, Your Majesty. I have such a nasty cold that I cannot smell anything!"

And that is how clever Fox saved her life.

Mowgli and Baloo's Lessons

Baloo, the big brown bear, was teaching Mowgli the Law of the Jungle. There was so much to learn that Mowgli sometimes got things wrong and Baloo would tell him off with a gentle cuff around the ears.

Mowgli had just been in trouble again, and he stormed off and hid in the trees.

"Don't be so hard on him, my old friend," said Bagheera, the black panther, who had been watching the lesson from the cover of the long grass.

"He needs to learn, so he doesn't come to harm," grumbled Baloo. "At the moment I'm teaching him the Master Words of the Jungle that will protect him from all the jungle creatures. Come, little man cub, stop sulking, and show Bagheera what you know."

Mowgli slid down a tree trunk and made a face at Baloo.

"I'm only coming down for Bagheera," complained Mowgli. "The jungle has many tongues and I know them all." And he rattled off several of the jungle languages, happy to show off his language skills to Bagheera.

"One day I'll lead my own tribe, and we'll throw sticks and dirt at Baloo!" laughed Mowgli.

"Mowgli," growled Baloo. "You've been talking to the Monkey People. They're evil."

Sheepishly, Mowgli looked at Bagheera.

"It's true, man cub," said the wise panther. "They lie and cheat. They have no Law. Baloo is right, you must stay away from them."

Unbeknown to either Baloo or Bagheera, some of the Monkey People were hiding in the trees above. They waited until the three friends were asleep and then they grabbed Mowgli and swung him away through the treetops.

Mowgli was frightened. He knew that he had to get word back to his friends so they could rescue him. He saw Chil, the kite bird, circling above the trees and remembered Baloo's lessons. He called to the bird in his language.

"The Monkey People have kidnapped me and are taking me to their city. Tell Baloo and Bagheera."

Meanwhile, Baloo and Bagheera were running through the jungle looking for Mowgli. When they got Chil's message they headed for the ancient ruins that the Monkeys called their home. Before they got to the lost city, they came across Kaa, the python.

"What are you hunting?" hissed the snake.

"Monkey People, who have snatched Mowgli," explained Baloo.

"Ah, chattering, vain foolish things," sighed Kaa. "I'll help you."

At the ruined city, the Monkey People gathered around Mowgli.

"Teach us to be like man," they cried. "And we will be the wisest people in the jungle!"

Mowgli was wondering how he could escape, when Bagheera raced into the ruins, knocking down monkeys everywhere. But there were too many for the brave panther to fend off.

"Roll into the water tank," cried Mowgli. "They won't follow you there."

Bagheera lunged into the water tank just as Baloo arrived and took up the fight. Then Kaa pounced. He was everything the monkeys feared. They scattered with cries of "It's Kaa, run, run!"

Mowgli was free from the clutches of the terrible Monkey People.

"Little man, I'm so proud of you that you remembered the Master Words of the Jungle," cried Baloo, giving Mowgli a huge bear hug.

After that day, Mowgli always tried his best to remember everything Baloo taught him.

The Fox and the Cookie

One evening, a clever fox saw a crow sitting on a branch, high up in a tree. The crow had a delicious-looking cookie in his beak. The fox was feeling hungry.

He called up to the crow, "Dear crow, I hear that you have a wonderful voice. Will you sing a song for me?"

The crow was flattered to hear the fox's kind words. He opened his beak to sing, and the cookie dropped right into the fox's mouth.

The next day, the fox came across the crow again. This time, the crow had a big piece of cake in his beak.

The fox said, "Dear Crow, I didn't quite catch your beautiful singing yesterday. Could you sing again for me now?"

This time, the crow realized what the fox was up to. He put the cake safely in his nest, and then began to sing in an awful croaky voice.

The fox put his paws to his ears and never bothered the crow again.